CHES

FOLK TALES

CHESHIRE FOLK TALES

THE JOURNEY MAN

The History Press

First published 2012
Reprinted 2014

The History Press
The Mill, Brimscombe Port
Stroud, Gloucestershire, GL5 2QG
www.thehistorypress.co.uk

British Library Cataloguing in Publication Data.
A catalogue record for this book is available from the British Library.

ISBN 978 0 7524 6513 5

Typesetting and origination by The History Press
Printed in Great Britain

Contents

Foreword

This is a whole new experience for me and I have to say, it was with a mixture of pleasure and trepidation that I received the invitation to write a foreword to this book of Cheshire folk tales. Pleasure, of course, as I was flattered to be asked, but I cannot deny the feelings of doubt that rapidly followed as I realised that I now had to do something about it – but where to start? It is without question a subject dear to my heart. I have been involved with the folk culture of my home county of Cheshire for many years, and while my particular interest has been in the folk songs, music and traditions of the area, it soon became very clear that the two strands – song and story – are inextricably linked, forming the backbone of our local heritage and folklore.

These are the tales that were passed from person to person, generation to generation, for many years – in some cases centuries – and were often much more than mere entertainment. For many they defined a community. These stories belonged to the area and the people who lived there. They supported superstitious and religious beliefs – however outlandish they may seem to our modern ears – and gave an explanation for the things people did not fully understand. They provided life lessons in right and wrong, in what was good and what was evil.

Storytellers would enthral listeners, giving them a rare opportunity to escape into another world, exercise their imagination and involve themselves in thrilling adventures.

Soon others would start to learn these tales and pass them on as best they could. As all the material was transferred by word of mouth, the stories would be constantly developing, adapting and changing. Some things may have been misremembered or misheard, names and places might have been changed to make them more familiar and meaningful, and gaps may have been filled or a story extended. Some might even have been put into verse and sung as a folk ballad – a song telling a story.

Eventually, a large number of these tales were collected and written down. Many of those that had been adapted into songs were collected without their original melodies and were published in collections of verse. Others were adapted and the stories developed into more literary pieces, or were used as the basis for other works. William Shakespeare was one of many who used folk culture as a source of ideas and inspiration.

As the stories that Shakespeare adopted are still being told today (*King Lear*, *The Taming of the Shrew* and *Romeo and Juliet* – to name but a few) so these Cheshire tales have been allowed to develop in the time-honoured way of the oral tradition to meet the needs of a new audience. This is not history to be left in a dusty tome on a shelf; it is vibrant, alive and constantly changing. It should be out there being passed on from storyteller to storyteller, developing and growing as it goes. If, however, you don't have immediate access to a first-class storyteller, you might find these pages the next best thing.

Roy Clinging, 2012

ACKNOWLEDGEMENTS

It would be impossible to name all those who have helped me as I gathered tales for this book over the years, but I would like to acknowledge the great generosity and assistance that many have given me. I have chatted to old folk over tea, with people in the pubs, forestry wardens, librarians, curators, local historians, vicars, walkers, archaeologists and other storytellers. I am also indebted to those cataloguers from the past, whose works remain as a record of the local tales of their time.

I must also mention the three organisations that started me on the road to collecting Cheshire folk tales some four years ago. Thank you to Harthill Trust, Habitats and Hillforts, and The Woodland Trust, who all commissioned me to investigate and retell stories based on the Sandstone Ridge, Cheshire woodland and many other local features. The work that you all set me on made a great start in forming this collection.

Introduction

In writing any collection of folk tales, there will be a whole host of difficult decisions, but with Cheshire I had to decide first of all where qualifies as Cheshire. The county boundaries have moved a lot over the years; places such as Warrington were in Lancashire at one time, then later in Cheshire and now under their own unitary authority. More recently, the county has been split up into the Wirral, Halton, Cheshire West & Chester, and Cheshire East. In the end, as this is a collection of folk tales, I decided that I would revert back to the traditional boundaries of the county, those that resonate in the folk memory of the place. Cheshire has affectionately been remembered as a county shaped like a teapot. The Wirral Peninsula forms the spout, the south bank of the River Mersey wiggles along to make the lid, there is a long handle reaching out to Tintwistle, and the body of the pot drops down to touch on Staffordshire and Shropshire. Sadly, these boundaries leave out Warrington, which is a place that could do with a book of its own. For tales associated with the place, look up the books of local storyteller Wally Barnes. But this leads me to my second series of decisions.

Having marked out the map, I was amazed at how many folk stories were contained within these borders. There is something parochial about both the urban and rural communities of Cheshire, which means that almost every town, village and hamlet, every stone feature and waterway, has its own tales and folklore. Some are, of course, repetitions of a basic theme, but many are unique to their location. I could easily fill three or four books with Cheshire folk tales and so I have had to carefully choose what to include in this collection. My choices were made based on a number of criteria:

- Does it make a good story?
- Which are the classic tales of Cheshire that should be included?
- Which stories are being forgotten and will soon be lost?
- Which characters are found all over the county?
- Which stories help to sum up the history and spirit of Cheshire?

I am sure there will be a number of readers who will find some of their favourite local tales are not included. However, I hope that there will be tales here that readers have not heard before, or have not heard for a long time.

Of course, as a storyteller I tend to elaborate the original tale. I often refer to myself not so much as a guardian of folklore, but as a purveyor of fakelore. Although, this book being what it is, I have tried to keep as close to the original tales as I can. But bear in mind my natural leaning, especially as I retell these tales for today's audience. The challenge here is, of course, that many local tales are fragmentary. People will often give you a single sentence about a stone, or a couple of lines about a local ghost. At times there is very little actual story. My job as the storyteller is to try to string these recollections together to create some sort of narrative, which will be fun to follow, and that will help to illuminate the landscape. That is where my fakelorist nature comes in. An example of this would be the chapter called 'The Devil's Stony Features'. The Devil is blamed for many of the rocky features round the county. I have retold these as episodes in one long tale, which is essentially invented, but presents authentic Cheshire lore within an enjoyable framework.

Having so many stories in this county, I have managed to keep others in by placing a number within other stories. In 'Mermaids and Mere-maids', I tell the story of the Black Rock mermaid whilst the characters within the tale recall the Combermere Bells, the mermaid of Rostherne and the asrai. In this case, I wanted to create a sense of stories being shared amongst the local people, within families and such like, because this is how tales and folklore have been perpetuated over the generations. I have also included a number of references to local traditions, beliefs and a handful of words from the Cheshire dialect. Some of the stories are also from Cheshire folk songs. All this has been my attempt to paint a picture of the county's rich heritage, which is resisting oblivion despite the dramatic changes in its population since the Second World War. That said, you will see how Cheshire began as a mixed corner of the kingdom of Mercia in my tales of Ethelfleda and Canute, and this has continued pretty much throughout its history. This is exemplified by a quote from an election campaign in Northwich in the 1880s: 'My father was Swiss, my mother was a Manxwoman, I was born in Liverpool, and my nurse was Welsh. Is that Cheshire enough for you?'

So, despite the mixed backgrounds of the people who have come to live in Cheshire (I am from Sussex myself) it seems that the stories do remain, and it's now up to us to keep them alive. Over the years, a number of authors have grown up or lived locally, and used these folk tales as their inspiration. The most well known in recent times would be Alan Garner with *The Weirdstone of Brisingamen*, and the many other books that followed. Garner helped to raise a strong interest in the folklore of east Cheshire, and whenever I travel about the country people mention Alderley Edge and Garner's work. With such knowledge of east Cheshire being fairly well established then, I have chosen to focus more on west Cheshire in this collection, whilst still referring to the east with the likes of Congleton and 'The Wizard of Alderley Edge'.

Other famous works from the county include *Alice's Adventures in Wonderland*, *Sir Gawain and the Green Knight*, Elizabeth Gaskell's *Cranford*, and Roger Lancelyn Green's collection *The Adventures of Robin Hood*. And finally, there is now my collection, which I tentatively place on the shelf next to all those other references to Cheshire. All of us have been heavily influenced by the landscape of this amazing county. You can read this book from cover to cover, and there is a sense of progression in the order I have placed the stories. However, each tale can stand alone and you will not lose anything by dipping in and out of the book. But my hope is that this new collection of tales inspires you to get out there and see the mythical sights for yourself. Then to go on and tell the stories to whoever will listen; you'll be keeping our rich lore alive and also enjoying a good story.

The Journey Man, 2012

One

The Lady of the Mercians

Let me begin on the very edges of Mercia, where now there stands a bridge linking the Saxon south bank of Runcorn to the Viking north bank of Widnes. Together these towns are now known collectively as Halton. Alongside the familiar road bridge stands an older railway crossing, built in the style of castle towers and once known as the Ethelfleda Bridge. It seems a shame that Britain's once great warrior queen has been forgotten. The bridge is not only named in her honour, but it was designed to mirror Ethelfleda's fortress that once stood watching over the River Mersey, one of many burhs she had erected to guard over the wilder edges of her kingdom.

Let me then tell the tale of the Lady of the Mercians, beginning with her father. This is the king who, despite all of his great feats, became better known for burning some cakes. This is still often the case when someone burns the toast. He was, of course, Alfred the Great, the champion of the English, who, in Cheshire, is best remembered as the father of Ethelfleda. From a very young age, this gutsy young princess had shown that she wasn't like the other girls. Her mother, Ealswitha, had always hoped that she would be sent to a convent. This would be a safe haven where she would live with the nuns, being taught how to lead a virtuous life and develop the art of embroidery. Alfred, however, had seen something else in his daughter. She had an edge. She was a fighter. And so he decided that a convent was not the place for her. No, she would stay with him, along with her brother Edward, and they would learn to be great warriors together. After all, Alfred's kingdom was constantly under threat from those people from over the sea – despite the fact that the Saxons had originally come from overseas themselves. But then I guess they had set the example and now had to deal with those who were following. Who then would protect the English, Alfred's Anglo-Saxons, once he had gone? Better to have two young protectors than rely on one, simply because he was male.

And so Ethelfleda, together with her brother, grew into a fine warrior – a master of the seax, as all good Saxon warriors should be. Her mother was not happy, however. Ealswitha had relented on the convent idea, but her daughter should still be married. Agreeing with his wife on this, Alfred looked about for a suitable husband. What he wanted was a man he could trust. He needed someone that he knew would protect the kingdom and be a good match for his warrior princess. In the end, Alfred chose Ethelred, who not only had a similar name to his daughter but was a fellow campaigner in the cause of the English. The two men had fought together in many battles and so there was a great bond of trust between them. It was therefore agreed that Ethelfleda would marry Ethelred, and so the wedding was arranged.

Many were pleased to hear of this union, and news of it spread across the kingdom and beyond its borders. And then the news of the proposed marriage reached the ears of the Danes, those long-standing enemies of Alfred the Great; they were not so happy. They could see that such a partnership would only serve to make the kingdoms of the Anglo-Saxons stronger. They decided that something should be done to destroy this union, and when better to do this than at its beginning – on the wedding day itself.

The marriage ceremony went by smoothly, and Ethelfleda and Ethelred were joined in holy matrimony. The happy couple rode home, lord and lady side by side. And following on behind them was their entourage of soldiers, servants and maids-in-waiting. The two newlyweds were unaware that in the trees that lined that road, there was an army waiting for them. The Danes crouched in the leaves with their sharpened swords, ready to leap on the unsuspecting couple. It would be an ambush that would cut up the union sanctioned by the king. They would slice it apart before it could be consumated.

A fierce cry rose from the tree tops and out of those leaf-laden branches a ferocious band of Danish warriors descended, intent on killing the lord, his lady, and all who got in their way. Immediately, Ethelred told his lady to turn and ride away to safety, which she did, taking her maids-in-waiting with her. Meanwhile, the brave Ethelred turned to face the Danes together with his soldiers, all with their seaxes drawn – those deadly blades that gave the Saxons their name. As Ethelfleda rode frantically to safety, she turned to see how the battle was progressing, and saw that her husband and his band were not faring well. The Danes seemed to be gaining the upper hand as they continued to pour from the surrounding woodland. It would not be long until Ethelred would be overcome, and Ethelfleda could not run away knowing her husband's life was in the balance. So she pulled on the reins, turned her horse around and rallied her maids-in-waiting. Together, the women galloped back along the road to join the men in the battle. A bloody skirmish ensued; Ethelfleda and her ladies surprised the Danes with their presence , and then took advantage of their shock, plunging their seaxes forward and back into the hearts and guts of their enemies. Soon the Danes were too depleted to continue. Many turned and ran back through the trees in the hope of living another day.

Blood-splattered and sweaty, Ethelred turned to see his deliverer, his wife Ethelfleda. He knew then that he had a truly remarkable woman on his hands. Some say that the battle took place at Maiden Castle, Bickerton, where the happy couple had stopped for a rest on their way home. And so the hillfort received its name, in memory of the maids-in-waiting who, together with their lady, stood against the Danes. They showed those invaders how an Anglo-Saxon woman can give as good as any Anglo-Saxon man, and we've been learning that lesson again and again ever since.

Two

Ingimund's Saga

Together Ethelred and Ethelfleda ruled the kingdom of Mercia, but as Ethelred was much older than Ethelfleda, he eventually became too jaded to take such an active role. It was therefore his formidable wife, the young Lady of the Mercians, who effectively ruled the land. And it was during this time that a deputation of bedraggled Norsemen came to her asking for some land.

These were an exiled Nordic people led by Ingimund. They had sailed many miles, from one part of Britain to another, in search of somewhere to make their home. You see they were no longer welcome in Norway, not since Harald the Fine Hair had become the first king of that country. He had subdued the people as Harald the Mop-head, vowing before God that he would not cut his hair until he had become king of the whole land. In doing so, he had hoped that he might win the hand of Gytha, a fair but feisty young woman who knew what she wanted in a man. So, once he had achieved this task and cut his hair, Gytha became his queen, and all those who did not agree with Harald's rule were put out of the kingdom. And so Ingimund and his ragtag band of followers set off in their longships to find a new home. They sailed across the North Sea and round the tip of Scotland with the hope of making a new life in the Viking settlement of Dublin. But when they arrived, they found that it was the wrong time for Vikings. The Irish were throwing these foreigners out and reclaiming their land, so Ingimund ended up gaining more followers. It was a larger band for him to lead, but still they had no home.

They decided to try Wales; Ingimund hoped that the little island of Anglesey would be out of the way and free of trouble. But, as Ingimund and his company crossed the Irish Sea, the Welsh saw their ships, and fearing the worst they lined the beaches with warriors. They were headed by their king and readied themselves with their weapons gleaming in the sun. It was clear to Ingimund that this was not going to be their home either.

'But, where to now?' he thought. The longships slowly edged round the coast of Wales until they finally came to the Wirral Peninsula. After landing their ships, a tired and sorry-looking band of men set out to find whoever ruled the land, so that they might ask for somewhere to live.

It was this bedraggled group then that appeared before Ethelfleda, the Saxon Queen of Mercia, asking if there might be somewhere they could call home, having shared their sorry story. Ethelfleda looked at them with suspicion. She, her husband, her father and her brother had spent many years protecting their land from Vikings. Admittedly their greatest enemies were the Danes and these were Norsemen, but at the end of the day they were all Vikings. She decided therefore that she would let them live where they had landed – the northern half of the Wirral Peninsula – where they would be out of the way. This wasn't the best land in the kingdom either, by a long way, and so she was not giving away anything too valuable. Giving thanks, Ingimund and his Nordic brothers set off to make their new home in the northernmost part of Mercia. And so many places in the region gained Viking names, such as Wallasey, Leasowe, Greasby, Raby and Tranmere. But it was a boggy, marshy land and often riddled with midges. It was not a great place for farming either and it was a long journey to the market towns where they could trade. So, many of the Norsemen started to wish they lived somewhere else. Somewhere like Chester would be good, they thought, where there was a harbour and a market and a city wall. So a great gathering of the Wirral Norsemen was called, an assembly which those Vikings call a Thing. The area where this took place is now known as Thingwall, and it was here that there was a great debate and the plan to move to Chester was discussed in depth. Finally, Ingimund proposed that they should go to Chester peaceably at first, saying, 'Let us approach the city beseeching of the people that they let us join them in peace.' Then, seeing the desperation on the faces of his people, 'But should they refuse then we will take that city of Chester by force, driving the people from their homes and making it our own.' And a cheer rose up from the Norsemen. All were in agreement, and whether it was by request or by force, they would finally be settling in a new home.

Taking their helmets and shields and swords, should they need them, the Wirral Norsemen began to march down the Wirral towards the walled city of Chester. And it was not long until the lookouts on the wall saw them – a great band of Vikings, armed and marching towards their city. The people panicked, believing they were under attack, but what should they do?

A messenger was sent to Ethelfleda, their queen, in the hope that she would protect them. The queen heard of the people's plight and sighed. She had been right not to trust those Norsemen; they were just the same as their Danish cousins. And so the queen devised a plan for the people of Chester.

'Open your gates wide,' she said, 'so that the Norsemen think you are welcoming them in. But have all your people armed and waiting in hiding. Once the Vikings come in through the gates, close them as quick as you can. They will be surprised and trapped, and you will be able to kill them all.'

The messenger rushed back to the people of Chester with the plan and they put it into action. Ingimund and the Norsemen arrived and found the city gates to be open. Their hope initially had been to come in peace, and it seemed that the people of

Chester were willing to talk. With great expectation, the Vikings walked into the city, which seemed very quiet for a market day. No sooner were the Vikings inside than the gates started to close behind them. There was a cry from those who were at the rear of the crowd, shouting that it was a trap. This was confirmed by a cry from the Chester Saxons, who leapt out to attack the invaders. Before the gates could close, the Norsemen had turned. They were not going to allow themselves to be shut inside and slaughtered. A number of Ingimund's men lost their lives in the skirmish, but most escaped and they ran from Chester to regroup and make new plans.

The people of Chester were delighted with themselves, and slapped each other on the back, telling of how brave each of them had been in seeing off a ferocious Viking horde.

But Ingimund and his people were not happy. They had come to Chester in openness and they had been tricked. It was time therefore to put the second part of their plan into action – to take that city by force, driving its people from their homes and making it their own. And so they readied themselves for battle; a battle they knew would be hard. The people of Chester would be ready for them now and the gates would be closed, but the Vikings were used to climbing over walls.

With their helmets on, their shields strapped to their arms, their swords unsheathed and carrying their ladders, the Wirral Norsemen began to march down the Wirral towards the walled city of Chester again. And it was not long until the lookouts on the wall saw them again – a great band of Vikings, armed and carrying ladders, marching towards their city. The people panicked, they were under attack, but what should they do?

A messenger was sent to Ethelfleda, their queen, in the hope that she would protect them again. The queen heard of the people's plight and sighed. She could see that these Norsemen were just as persistent as their Danish cousins. And so the queen devised another plan for the people of Chester.

'As the Vikings climb up the walls,' she said, 'throw rocks and bricks down on them. Any rubble you can find in the city.

Or take any stone you have, remove it from some of your least valued buildings if necessary. Throw them down on those Vikings. See if they can climb up their ladders whilst you are pelting them with stone.'

The messenger rushed back to the people of Chester with this plan and they put it into action. As the Norsemen climbed the hill on which the city sat, and as they placed their ladders against its walls, the people of Chester waited. Then, as the attackers climbed up, the people of Chester began to throw down their rocks and bricks and stones. The Norsemen were hit in the face, in the back, on the fingers, and they also began to fall. As one fell, he would fall on top of another Viking climbing the ladder below him. And as they were starting to make a heap of moaning, bruised and broken Vikings, the shower of stones continued. Ingimund and his men were not going to remain here. So they ran from Chester to regroup and make new plans.

Again the people of Chester revelled in their victory and slapped each other on the back, telling of how brave each of them had been in seeing off a ferocious Viking horde.

Now Ingimund and his people were not happy. They had come to Chester to make a new home, and they were not going to be stopped now. If they could not climb over the walls, then maybe they could enter Chester by going under the walls. With their helmets on, their shields strapped to their arms, their swords unsheathed, the Wirral Norsemen began to march down the Wirral again, towards the walled city of Chester. This time, however, they brought with them screens of willow and poles made from branches, together with a host of digging tools. And it was not long until the lookouts on the wall saw them again – a great band of Vikings, armed and carrying a host of things, marching towards their city. The people were ready with their stones, but it didn't look like their enemies were going to be climbing the walls again. This time, the people of Chester watched before they panicked.

The Vikings held their screens above their heads as protection from any tumbling stones and gathered below the city walls.

Then they used their poles to hold up the screens, making shelter for themselves all round the base of the walls. The people of Chester were now worried. All they had were stones. Some started to throw them down on to the Vikings, but it was no good. The screens protected the invaders who were now starting to dig into the hill, hoping to make their way under the walls and into the city.

The people of Chester panicked. How could they stop this attack? An attack from underneath. A messenger was sent to Ethelfleda, their queen, in the hope that she would protect them again. The queen heard of the Vikings' new plan and she sighed again. These Norsemen were more intelligent than their Danish cousins. And so the queen devised another plan for the people of Chester.

'I know my people are fine brewers of ale,' she said, 'now take all the ale you have in the city and boil it up. Make fires on the walls themselves for you to boil the beer. Then when it is bubbling and spitting, when it is at its hottest, tip the vats of ale down over the walls on to those Vikings. Let's see whether those screens of theirs offer protection against liquid rather than stone.'

The messenger rushed back to the people of Chester with this plan and they put it into action. Some gathered the ale that was in the city, while others built fires on the walls. Then as the beer boiled and spat, they carefully carried the great vats to the battlements and tipped the scalding hot liquid over and on to the Norsemen. The screens were only meant to protect them from large objects, such as rocks and bricks, not beer. And the intensely hot, steaming ale tumbled on to the Vikings, who screamed as they were burnt and scalded. Some say it was so hot that the very flesh of some Norsemen fell from their bodies. And so the boiling shower continued. Ingimund and his men were not going to remain there. They ran from Chester to regroup and make new plans.

Oh, how the people of Chester were full of themselves. They slapped each other on the back, telling of how brave each of them had been seeing off a ferocious Viking horde.

Now Ingimund and his people were getting angry. Chester would be theirs no matter what. If the people were going to throw down boiling beer and not rocks, then they would waterproof their screens and continue to dig until they had made their way into the city under its walls.

With their helmets on, their shields strapped to their arms, their swords unsheathed, the Wirral Norsemen began to march down the Wirral again, towards the walled city of Chester. They had new screens with them this time. Screens with the added extra of animal hide to waterproof them. And the lookouts on the city walls saw them again – the band of Vikings, armed and carrying screens again. The people were already stoking up the fires to boil the vats of ale again. But when the Vikings set up their screens, the people looking from the walls could see they were different. They were covered with animal hide and that meant the boiling beer would not penetrate to scald the Vikings. And so the people of Chester panicked. A messenger was sent to Ethelfleda, their queen, in the hope that she would protect them again. Her plans had seen the Vikings off three times before, but here they were back again and they had already started the tunnels. How soon would it be until they were beyond the walls and up into the city? The queen heard of the Vikings' modifications and she sighed a long sigh. These Norsemen were clever, very clever. They could show the Danish a thing or two. And so the queen devised yet another plan, the final plan for the people of Chester.

'I know my people are fine beekeepers,' she said, 'now take all the hives you have in the city and carefully carry them up on to the walls. Then throw them down on to the screens that protect those Vikings. Throw all your hives over the walls and on to your enemies.'

The messenger hesitated and said, 'My lady, the screens stopped the rocks and stones and now they are waterproof. I do not believe that wicker hives will penetrate the screens.'

'The hives may not, but the little warriors contained inside will,' answered Queen Ethelfleda.

The messenger rushed back to the people of Chester with this plan and they put it into action. They gathered all the wicker hives they could find in that city and carried them up on to the walls. Then, as each hive gave out a low hum, the people tossed them out over the battlements and down on to the Viking screens.

Ingimund and his men were digging furiously, knowing that they were protected from rocks and from ale. They knew too that these would not be a problem once they were under the walls. But as they dug they heard some strange noises. Firstly, there was a flopping sound as something soft landed on the screens. Not the crash of rocks. Not the splash of beer. It was one flop after another. Then there followed a droning, a low humming sound which gradually grew louder and louder and louder – until the hum of bees was joined by the screams of men. Thousands and thousands of angry bees suddenly surrounded the Vikings, each tiny warrior looking to sting the first living thing it found. Now you may be able to continue digging if rocks are falling around you. You may be able to keep going if boiling ale falls. But when you are surrounded by swarms and swarms of bees, you are not going to do anything else but run. Screaming and hopping and

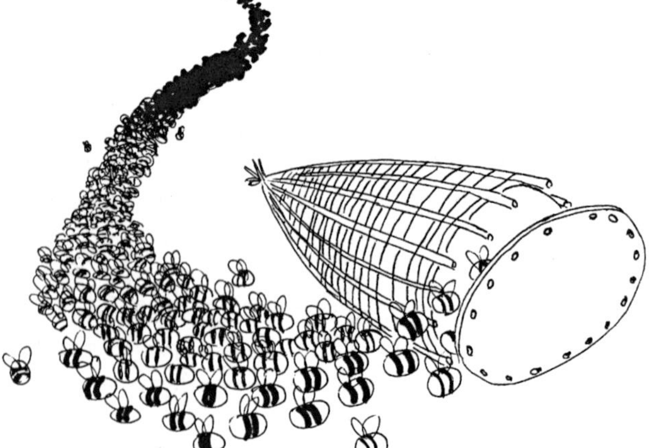

waving their arms and slapping their sides with screams and shrieks, the Norsemen dropped everything and ran. They ran from Chester and up on to the Wirral. They ran through the bogs and the marshes, all the way back to their makeshift homes where they sat and nursed their wounds. Maybe they would regroup and try Chester again, but not today. The bites of midges are not as bad as the stings of bees.

And the people of Chester were full of themselves. They slapped each other on the back, telling of how brave each of them had been in seeing off the ferocious Viking horde. However, they could not celebrate with a drink of ale and they did wonder where they would get more bees from. Still, they had seen off their enemies for today and it did not look as if they were coming back, thanks to the clever plans of their Queen, the Lady of the Mercians, Ethelfleda, daughter of Alfred the Great.

•

Three

Thor's Stone

There are many large stones round the county, and all of them have their stories. The local people once believed that stones grew like plants, with the largest being the most ancient. It was imagined that some of these giant rocks had watched the affairs of humanity as they worked the land and fought their battles. The stones, being the watchers over the ages, should not be moved but ploughed round, and left to continue their endless vigil.

Standing at the northern end of the Wirral Peninsula, hidden between the bending trees and boggy floor of Thurstaston Common, there is an enormous red sandy stone. This is Thor's Stone, from which the common takes its name. In the days of Ingimund, this location would have felt hundreds of miles from anywhere. The Wirral Peninsula juts out from the main body of Cheshire like a finger reaching out into the sea, a desperate attempt maybe to connect with distant lands and foreign people. Separated from both Wales and Liverpool by the rivers Dee and Mersey, the Wirral carries on its back Thor's Stone, which stood proudly in the heart of these Viking lands. Over the years, tales have grown up, twisting about themselves like the trees that surround this great rock. Theories and stories cling to it like a moss, yet the secrets of its past remain hidden to us, lying down, sunken deep in the black boggy land of that place.

It is said that the Vikings themselves placed the great rock to commemorate their tremendous battle at Bromborough. It is so large though that it may be more likely that Thor himself placed it there. Together, god and Viking celebrated their victory with this enormous feature, standing as a solid reminder of their might. Here then began an ever-growing chain of sacrifices, so they say. A long line of victims were brought to this immense altar to ensure continual victory for the disciples of Thor. With the footsteps of captors and of priests forcing their victims up the crude steps, so the stone's hard edges were smoothed. As their blood spilt on to the stone it was absorbed, staining that rock over the years. And now it stands a bald but deep red stone, coloured by its people's determination to take more of Mercia. A people who continued their dark rituals in this hidden corner; tucked away in the woodland on the edge of everywhere.

Years later, when England had been forged, and the Vikings had dispersed and intermarried with the local people, the magic of Thor's Stone remained strong. The rituals had run deep into the local collective consciousness and even children recognised the stone's magical qualities. Known as the Fair Maiden's Hall, children would come each year to dance about the rock. In that moment, they embodied the more gentle fairy-like spirits of that place, spirits of mischief and jollity – a significant contrast to the Viking rituals of destruction and domination. Morris Men come on Midsummer's Night to dance their celebration of the sun at its greatest strength. And so it seems that Thor himself has settled down, as his people have now found peace in these lands. Of course, there is the occasional rumble of anger, memories of the past heard in the thunderous storms rolling in from the sea and over the plain. But generally, he is calmer, happy to be remembered by a smooth, red stone, visited by fascinated walkers and climbed over by children and teenagers.

Four

Edward's Little City

Ethelfleda had a brother who was known as Edward the Elder. It was his plan to unite the kingdoms of England and continue his father's vision, one nation under one king. On her death at Tamworth, Ethelfleda had named her daughter, Elfwyn, to be her successor and ruler over the kingdom of Merica. Elfwyn, sadly, was not as strong as her mother and she succumbed to her uncle's designs on her kingdom. Therefore Edward, the ruler of Wessex, took over Mercia as well as East Anglia and Essex and continued to push hard against the Danes in the north and east.

Now, it was on the northern marches of Mercia, along the River Mersey, that Edward the Elder feared attack from his enemies. His sister had built a burh at Runcorn, which oversaw all those who were entering the River Mersey from the sea, but what about further down the river? There was a small village about 10 miles inland, and it was here that Edward saw how easily his enemies could cross the river without anyone looking out for them. What was needed then was a fortress, or something more impressive – a city – where he could station his knights. They would be ready for any attack along this stretch of the northern marches, but just their presence would be a sure deterrent. Looking about, Edward saw that there was much woodland round the place. This would provide cover for his enemies' forces, but if he was to have the trees felled not only would he clear the land for an unobstructed view, but here also were materials to help fortify the settlement. He then gave orders for those trees to be cut down and for the timber to be used to build a large wooden wall. Once the wall was up, Edward brought in his knights – and the settlement, which was once a small farming village, became a mediaeval city. It had fortifications and its own armed protectors. And so it stood, Britain's smallest city, proud on a hill surrounded by a sea of tree stumps – a clear view all about, making a surprise attack impossible. It was named Thelwall, because of the wall of felled trees, and became known as Edward the Elder's Little City. This city status is still celebrated on the walls of the village's pub, the Pickering Arms, where its states: 'In the year 923 King Edward the Elder founded a city here and he called it Thelwall.'

Five

King Canute in Cheshire

Many may have heard of the great king, Canute – more accurately spelt Knut – as it was he who brought all three lands under one king; they being Denmark, Norway and England. What Alfred, Ethelfleda, Ingimund and Edward the Elder would have made of this, I do not know. After all their years of troubles, Canute, a Dane, became king of them all.

Now, it was whilst the king was travelling across the land of England to defend it from the Scots that he entered Mercia. He and his army were soon confronted by the River Lily. It was a great waterway, but one which needed to be crossed all the same, and so soldiers were sent to find a suitable point at which to ford the river. They soon found a place where the banks of the river were very flat and sandy. Canute led his army through the soft sand and, splashing through the shallow channel, on to the opposite bank. It was on that bank that Canute then had that horrible uncomfortable feeling of damp sand in his shoes. There were more miles to march over yet and he could not march with his feet in this way. So, he found a place on the bank on which to sit. There he took off his shoes to empty them of the annoying sand. There was more there than he had first thought and so he poured it out on to the sandstone floor beneath him, making a snaking pattern as he did so.

Now, at this moment, a wedding party appeared in the neighbouring lane, making their way from the local church. On seeing such a happy party of people, Canute called out to wish the married couple well.

'May you be blessed with as many children as there are grains of sand falling from my shoes!' he said, holding them aloft in each hand.

Everyone laughed at the sight in good humour, and thanked the king for his kind wishes. The couple told many people of this chance encounter and what the king had been up to. So much so that soon a new tradition developed within the town. As a way of wishing well to visitors and celebrating events, the people of the town began to make pictures out of sand. Using a cone, they would pour the sand out into shapes in front of their houses, with messages wishing well to folk. This became known as sanding and is unique to this town, which is called Knutsford. Queen Victoria is known to have commented on the practice when she visited the town and photos of it still exist. Many of the messages resemble King Canute's first respects to that married couple, saying:

> Long may they live, and happy may they be,
> Blest with content and misfortune free.

However, Canute did not stop in the town, as he had Scotland to get to. It may have been on this campaign, that he heard many of his advisers and soldiers talking of how great he was. After all, he was the first to unite and rule over the kingdoms of England, Denmark and Norway. And it looked as if soon Scotland would be his also, and what of Wales? Ireland? Or even Sweden?

'Sire,' they said, 'is there no one who can stop you? You are mighty and all that you turn your attention to becomes yours. Why, even the wind and the waves would be calmed at your voice.'

'Yes,' said others, 'if you would tell the tide to stop, it would cease in its path and turn back.'

Now Canute liked to hear this talk and decided to see for himself how far his authority spread. Would he truly be able to tell the tide to stop? Would the sea indeed turn back?

It was in Mercia that Canute chose to test the extent of his authority, but the only access to the sea which could be found was that at the northernmost point of the Wirral Peninsula. A place reminiscent in some ways of Scandinavia, with its wide flat beaches and bright skies reaching far overhead – a place where the oceans open up before you, calling you to adventure in new lands. Canute and his entourage headed off to this northernmost point, carrying a makeshift throne with them. After all, Canute would be taking on the mighty sea, and any additional sign of his authority would surely not go amiss.

The throne was placed on the rocks at Leasowe Bay, and King Canute took his seat. The sea, as if aware of the royal challenge, started to rise. It is known, of course, that the tide can rise quickly along that coast. The sun was covered by a great black cloud and a cold wind started to sweep in from the frozen north to chill the bones of the king. As his robes started to flap, Canute was aware that he was facing the power of nature, the power of the wind and the waves. He was suddenly aware of his own humanity. A great king he might be, but no matter how great, he was still only a man. He was also aware that his advisers and soldiers were watching, safe up on the rocks, keen to see him order the sea to turn back. Foolishly, Canute raised his hand and called out as best he could against the rising wind, 'Sea, come not hither!'

The waves ignored him and there was a rush of salt water up on to the rocks, a splash glancing across the king's cheek. Then as the waves pulled back, gathering for a further assault, Canute, arm raised, called out again, 'Sea, come not hither!'

Again the salty water crashed forward, this time a little further and a little higher. Canute could see that soon the waters would be rising up over the rock on which his throne was set. He tried a third time: 'Sea, come not hither!'

And remembering how the water would soon be up on to the rocks, he added, 'Nor wet the sole of my foot!'

This time it was as if the wind and the sea had lost patience with Canute's pathetic orders. A great gust came, almost whisking the crown off the king's head and wrapping his cloak about his face. The sea charged forward and crashed about Canute, not only wetting the sole of his foot but soaking his legs and robes with a cold, stinging saltiness.

'Enough!' shouted Canute, staggering to his feet and attempting to push the cloak from his face. 'Enough!' he shouted, but not to the sea this time, to his advisers and soldiers.

Slipping and sliding up from the rocks, he called out to his men to stop standing there gawping in disbelief, and to help him up on to dry land.

Breaking their trance, the men leapt down the rocks to help their king, providing him with a fresh cloak, some robes and a pair of shoes, but they were unable to speak. They had hoped to see the full extent of their king's authority, a great event to tell their grandchildren, but it seemed the full extent of his powers was not so great after all. Sensing their disappointment, Canute told them all that they were fools to think he could command the forces of nature. He may be a great king, one who had authority over three nations, but he was only a man. They must remember that all kings are merely human, humans placed in seats of great responsibility by God, but not gods themselves to be followed blindly. And on hearing these words, the advisers and the soldiers did feel a little foolish for their previous expectation. They again saw their king as a good and wise man, their teacher as well as their lord. Of course, Canute was not the ruler of three nations for nothing. A great leader knows how to turn a situation around, knows how to be a king of spin.

And there on the rocks at Leasowe Castle a throne did stand, said to have been Canute's, with the words carved into the back of it: 'Sea, come not hither, nor wet the sole of my foot.' Sadly, I hear that it was vandalised some eighty years ago and so no trace of it remains, but if you stand there on

those rocks, it is easy to imagine Canute looking out to sea, attempting to hold sway over the tide. So, the story of Canute continues to be told and is probably the one thing that most people remember of this remarkable king.

Six

The Runaway Prince of Mercia

As far as local saints are concerned, I could tell of St Werburgh or I could speak of St Chad. Both of these saints are celebrated in Cheshire, with Werburgh being the patron for Chester Cathedral and churches dedicated to St Chad appearing all over the county. However, both of these saints lived in the days when this was all Mercia and their ministries took them far and wide, with Chad becoming the Bishop of York and opening monasteries in Lichfield. Yet neither of them ventured too far into this northern end of the kingdom. The further north they went, the wilder these borderlands became. Access from the sea, and the far reach of the River Mersey, meant that these lands were more prone to invasion from outside forces. Then there were the Danes who were pressing in from the north-east. Now, I am not suggesting that these saints would not be up for a challenge. However, their own call was probably a more pastoral one; working amongst their own flock was perhaps a better use of their time. I would therefore like to tell of a lesser-known saint, one who has become part of the folklore of these lands and whose miracle actually took place in Cheshire. For me, he is far more interesting, not only being somewhat mysterious (it is hard to ascertain who his father was, for instance), but also being a very human saint. I would say he is the truly local saint for these more northern parts of Mercia, whilst even his name is uncertain. Is it Berteline or Bertoline? In Staffordshire he is known as Bertram. And then others have suggested Bartholomew. For the sake of ease, I like to simply refer to him as St Bert.

St Bert seems to have been first introduced to the people of northern Mercia by Ethelfelda, Lady of the Mercians, in the tenth century. As she built her line of burhs through her kindgom, she came to Stafford, where she came across a local cult dedicated to St Bert. There was something about this saint which attracted her, and so when she built her northernmost burh overlooking the River Mersey, she also ensured a church was built in the name of this saint. This little church later saw the founding of Norton Priory, which was built with both St Bert and St Christopher as its patrons. The latter, being better known, seems to have taken over and a great statue of Christopher has been found in the grounds of the priory. This is currently on display, but no such effigy of St Bert has been found. It is here then that I tell some of his story.

It begins long ago in Saxon Mercia, when a prince was so inspired by St Patrick's ministry in Ireland that he too wanted to make a name for himself. Rejecting his royal position, Prince Bert removed all signs of his status from his person, dressed in the sackcloth of a holy man and took a Bible from his father's chapel. He wandered north until he reached the banks of the River Mersey, the very edge of his father's kingdom. Here he found a small boat to set off in a westerly direction along the river, and into the Irish Sea. As he rowed out through the wind and the rain, he excitedly considered the prospect of all the wonders he would experience as a holy man. He could stand the splashing of the waves in his face, the flapping of his robes in the icy wind and the salt drying out his lips. Bert knew that all this would fade as he drove snakes from the kingdom and brought penitent kings to their knees.

He finally arrived on the beach in hope of some kind of welcome as he was cold, tired and hungry. He didn't need to wait long. A voice called out to him as he pulled his boat up on to the stony shore. It was a man armed with spear and sword, running along the rocks ordering Bert to stay where he stood.

'Who are you and why are you here?' demanded the soldier.

'I am a holy man who has come to bring the Gospel to your king.'

'Holy man, are you?' asked the armed man and he could see Bert's sackcloth robes. 'What do you have under there?' he said, pointing to a large square shape in the cloth with his sword.

'This is simply my Bible, the Word of God,' answered Bert, pulling out the great book.

'Then you must be a holy man. Welcome then, Father, to our shores. I will take you to our king, who is interested in the teachings of your Christ.'

Bert was pleased to hear these words. He would be welcomed and brought in to share food with the king before a warm fire no doubt. As he climbed up the rocks on to the grassy land, the soldier continued talking.

'Aye, it is good you are a holy man and not some prince. We are fed up with princes and kings coming over here from Britain, trying to take over our kingdom. No, you are a holy man and as such you are most welcome.'

'What would you have done to a prince?' asked Bert out of interest.

But the solider was not listening. Instead, he strode on, determined to lead Bert out of the wet wind and into the warm hall of his king.

Bert was pleased to be received by the king and all his hopes were fulfilled. Soon he was filling his stomach with warm food and sitting before a roaring fire in dry clothes. That was until the meal ended, when Bert was expected to teach the people. The king had ordered his soldiers to gather all those who lived thereabouts, be they servant, slave or free, and now the expectation was on Bert to regale them

with some of the teachings of Christ. And so, standing before the expectant crowd, he carefully opened the Bible and, taking a deep breath, began to read. To his surprise the people listened and so, growing in confidence, he continued reading. Now there was one particular person in the crowd who was listening especially carefully. She was sitting on the right of the king and fairly close to where Bert was standing. She did not need to listen so intently simply because she found him hard to hear. On the contrary, it was because she could hear him that she listened more closely, for she found his voice so soft and deep and appealing that he had captured her complete attention.

Once Bert had finished his reading, he closed the Bible and attempted a prayer which he had heard said many times in his father's chapel, and then he looked to the king. The king seemed pleased, the people had listened, and only one or two had fallen asleep. And so the king allowed Bert to stay and asked him to read to his people every day from then on.

Each day, the people would gather to hear Bert read, thinking he was teaching them. And each day, the young woman who had been sitting next to the king came and sat in her usual place and listened ever so intently. And as each day passed, Bert noticed how he had caught the attention of this one particular person, a quite beautiful person. And with each day, he would look at her more and more as he tried to read from the scriptures.

Of course she was the king's daughter and she was able to arrange secret meetings, and very soon she was receiving personal readings from Bert. And later those readings did not use words so much. In fact, you may say that they were more re-enactments than readings, and actions came to play a more important role in their time together than words. And soon there were no scriptures at all, but simply encounters of a divine and passionate love.

Until Bert said to the princess one night, 'Let us be married.'

'I cannot marry you,' she laughed, 'I am a princess and so I can only marry a prince.'

It was then Bert's turn to laugh, 'Then we can get married, for I am a prince.'

Now the princess stopped laughing, 'You are a dead man! If my father finds out you are a prince he will have you killed. Oh, why did you come here?' And she began to cry.

'I came to be a holy man, but now I am in love with you,' explained Bert.

What could the two of them do? After many ideas with many tears, the two of them decided to run away, to run away together and be married, in secret.

And so Bert ran away from another royal household, but this time it was not only with the Bible but a bride-to-be as well. The two of them found a chapel where a priest married them and then they headed down to the beach where Bert's boat had remained. Fearing for their lives if they remained in Ireland, the young couple clambered into the boat and set off for Britain. Rowing out across the Irish Sea, through the wind and the rain, Bert was excited at the prospect of returning to his father's kingdom with a beautiful princess as his wife. He could stand the splashing of the waves in his face, the flapping of his robes in the icy wind and the salt drying out his lips. Bert knew that all this would fade as he became a prince again and presented his new bride to his father, the King of Mercia.

They finally came to the mouth of the River Mersey and after some fighting against the current, Bert and his princess climbed out of the boat on to the riverbank. They were both hoping for a warm welcome, both being cold, tired and hungry. And they didn't need to wait long. A voice called out as they clambered up the bank and they saw a man armed with spear and sword leaping over the rocks and ordering them to stay where they stood.

'Who are you and why are you here?' demanded the soldier.

'I am Bert, Prince of Mercia. Take me to my father, your king.'

'Prince Bert!' gasped the armed man. 'What are you doing here!' he said, pointing his sword at him.

Bert was a little perturbed at this man's response.

'I have returned to my home, to my father's kingdom …'

'Then I must arrest you and take you to your father as prisoner,' stated the soldier.

Bert couldn't believe what he had heard.

'Yes,' continued the warden, 'when you discarded your royal position, the king was furious and ordered that if ever you were found on Mercia's lands you were to be arrested and brought to him where you will face your death.'

Bert was stunned and struggled for words. He explained that he had left Mercia to be a holy man. That he had married a beautiful Irish princess, but they could not remain in Ireland as the king there would have killed him. If what the soldier had said was true, then his wife had nowhere to go. And so he pleaded that the solider would not arrest him.

The soldier was not a cruel man and so said he would turn his back to Bert and his bride for just a few minutes. If he was to turn back and see that the two of them were no longer behind him, then he would believe this encounter to have been a dream. But if they were still in sight when he turned back, then he would arrest Bert and take him to his father and almost certainly to his death.

Bert tried to thank the soldier, who turned his back, but his wife pulled at his wrist and the two of them turned themselves around to run. They ran along the bank of the River Mersey first, but then soon turned southwards to head over the hills, desperately hoping that they would not meet any more of the king's guard and that the soldier had been true to his word.

For months, the couple wandered through the wilds of Merica. They survived on the kindness of strangers – few that they were in that bleak, desolate corner of the kingdom. Or they would hunt for food themselves, cooking on a makeshift fire and trying to find shelter for the night. Caves and logs became their temporary bedchambers. This was not the life that either Bert or the princess were accustomed to, and it was not the life of a holy man either. And it certainly wasn't a life for a pregnant woman. The princess was now expecting, and so the pressure to find somewhere they could stay without being recognised had suddenly grown.

It was as they were wandering over a long, curving ridge of hills that the princess had to stop. Their pace had slowed a lot, but now she could walk no further. Begging Bert to let her rest, they soon found a large cave where she could shelter. Bert then said that he would go to find food. He had seen a settlement down below the hills and hoped that the people there would be kind. It was, in fact, the village of Wetton. He and his princess bride had both wandered into the Peak District of what is now called Derbyshire.

Making his way to the first house, he pushed the door open slightly and called in. Suddenly, from out of the darkness a rough-faced man appeared and pushed Bert away from the door.

'What do you want, stranger?' he asked curtly.

'Please, I need help,' begged Bert, 'we are strangers here but we need food.'

'We all need food, boy,' the man growled.

'No, you don't understand,' Bert continued, 'my wife is pregnant. I must look after her. Is there nothing you could spare?'

The man within the house was not unkind and he could see the desperation in Bert's face as he stood there in the fading light of the day.

The man reached into the house and brought out three loaves of bread and looked about as he passed them over.

'Where is this wife of yours?' he asked.

'She is just over the hill there,' answered Bert as he pushed the three loaves into his bag. 'She is sheltering in a large cave. We may have to stay there tonight ...'

'No,' cried the man, 'you mustn't leave her there! That's Thor's Cave!'

Bert looked at the man confused.

'That cave,' continued the man, looking terrified, 'is the resting place of wolves. Get back there and get your wife out. Come back here if you have to, but get her out of there!'

Bert had not even said thank you and there was no chance of that now. He ran out of the settlement. He ran up over the hills. As he did so he could see that the moon had risen in the sky and the darkness was falling about him. He came to the other side of the hill and was about to run down to the cave, when a chilling howl echoed up to his ears. Other howls joined in and then in the light of the moon he saw the wolves coming out of Thor's Cave. They were sniffing about and stopping every so often to howl into the air. And on their lips he could see blood – blood dripping on to the ground, blood on the pieces of cloth which stuck to their fur.

'No!' shouted Bert, distraught deep within his soul, 'No!'

The wolves heard his cry and turned to face him. Then, growling, they began to walk towards him. Bert could not even go to the cave to see what remained of his wife and his unborn child. He turned and began to run up the hill again. The wolves gave chase and the echo of growls and howling bounced all about the slopes again.

Bert ran and ran, but the wolves soon caught the scent of some nearby sheep and turned away from the escaping prince to catch something easier. Still Bert ran and ran. Tears were now streaming down his face, as he continued to run. The terror of that night spurred him on. Running and running until he could neither walk nor cry any more, he fell to the ground.

It was on a small hill above a brook that Bert stopped, a breathless, pitiful pile of rags shivering in the small hours of the night. As he sat up and looked about him, all he could think about was how all his hopes and dreams had fallen apart. He had thrown away his position as a prince. He had destroyed his opportunity to be a holy man in Ireland. He was banished from his home by his own father. And now he had lost the one woman he had loved and their child.

'I wish I was dead!' he screamed out across the brook.

And it was at that point that someone who had been following him stepped out of the shadows. It was someone who had been following right from his very first attempts to be a holy man. It was that Old Urchin, the Devil.

'Ah, poor Bert,' he said mockingly. 'You so wanted to be a holy man but what happened? Made a few mistakes, did we?' the Devil chuckled.

Bert sighed. This was all he needed now. He turned away from the Devil to look at the brook.

'I'd say you did. Didn't really have that chastity thing sorted, did you?'

'Go away,' mumbled Bert.

'Ah, but Bertie, Bertie, Bertie,' continued the Devil, pretending to be concerned over the prince's shoulder, 'there's always a second chance. Let's see if you have it in you to be a real holy man ...'

Bert carried on trying to ignore him.

The Devil glanced down to where Bert was looking and saw three stones larger than many of the others, each about the size of a hand.

'Oh, see those three stones down there, Bertie boy. Let's see if you can turn them to bread shall we.' The Devil had tried this before, but then that was with Christ. Bert was small fry compared to the Son of God.

'Leave me alone,' Bert barked.

'Can't do it?' asked the Devil, with mock surprise. 'Go on, I bet you can. Give it a try. Turn the stones into bread.'

Bert shook his head and tried to ignore the Old Urchin, but he kept on and on. The Devil continued goading Bert, poking him and telling him he was no good, trying to get him to speak to the stones just so that he could do what the Devil asked, and then, when nothing happened, still look a fool.

On and on the Devil went until Bert could stand it no longer. He looked up to Heaven and cried out, 'God, help me!'

And when he did, the sun just seemed to peep over the horizon. The sky took on the slight glow of hope and a thought dawned in Bert's head. He remembered something in his bag.

'Devil,' he said, 'you can forget your stones, because I don't need to turn them into bread. I have these.' And turning to the Devil he pulled out the three loaves from his bag; the loaves that the man at Wetton had given him.

And as Bert showed them to the Devil, suddenly, before his eyes, three loaves of bread turned into stone – three loaf-shaped stones.

'Urh?' gasped a confused Devil. 'Bread into stone? Didn't I ask for stones into bread? Or was it bread into stone?'

The Devil couldn't remember which one he had asked for and a miracle had definitely taken place before him; but what kind of miracle? The Devil kept on repeating the words 'bread' and 'stone' over and over, trying to work out which one it was, until he was so confused he felt he couldn't stay. So, with a flap of his wings and a jump in the air, the Old Urchin disappeared.

And as the sun rose, Bert found himself laughing. The Devil had gone and now any food he did have had turned into stone. He placed the three stones on the hill, stood up and looked about. All of a sudden he felt as if all his troubles had rolled down that hill and into the brook. He felt that with this new day, there was a new start. So having journeyed north and east, and then travelled back to the west, Bert decided that it was probably time now to head south.

He walked for several days, considering all that had happened on that hill by the brook at Barthomley, until he came to another channel of water. This was more of a river – the River Sow. He saw that there was a small island in the middle of the river and Bert decided that's where he wanted to go. It could be his own island where he could be alone with his Bible, and where he could really reflect on everything that had happened to him so far. Walking along the bank of the

river, he soon found someone with a boat who was happy to take him over to the island. And on the way there, this stand-in ferryman asked Bert where he had come from. Bert then told him some of his story – not everything, as he was afraid of his father finding out that he was still in the kingdom. But he told him about losing his wife to the wolves and facing the Devil at Barthomley. When the boatman heard about the bread and the stones he was amazed.

'Why? We have a holy man here in our midst,' he exclaimed.

'No, no,' laughed Bert. 'I'm no holy man.'

'Hm,' said the boatman, eyeing the book that Bert was carrying. 'Why are you coming out here to this island?' he asked knowingly.

'To read the scriptures and reflect on what has happened in my life.'

'Then you are a holy man. You have seen miracles. You are withdrawing to a lonely place to read scriptures and meditate. Wait till my wife hears about this,' the boatman said assuredly.

Bert tried to dissuade the man from telling people. All he wanted was some peace and quiet. But it didn't take long for the people to start arriving. They wanted to learn from Bert, to hear of his encounter with the Devil, and to see if he had any other miracles up his sleeve.

Bert may not have been able to turn any more bread into stone, but he was a kind man at heart and learnt to love the people who came to visit him on his island. Together they built a church there and Bert erected a large wooden cross. Here he taught the people from the Bible and more and more people came to visit him.

Word of this holy man spread throughout the kingdom, and there are many other tales to tell of St Bert, but they are more for Staffordshire. So, I will bring this story to an end by saying that although Berteline gained interest from Queen Ethelfleda, he was soon forgotten. So much so that people wondered at those churches built in his name. It seems that no one knew of the name of Berteline and so it was suggested that it was a mistake; that, in fact, they were built in the name of Bartholomew, one of the twelve apostles. And so many of the churches' names were changed and St Berteline was almost lost. There are three churches to St Bartholomew in Cheshire, being in Church Minshull, Wilmslow and Great Barrow. There is a St Bartholomew's in Longnor, Staffordshire, but it is here where there is a statue of St Bert, one of the very few, with the title Evangelist to the Moorlands. And there is one image in stained glass of St Berteline in Cheshire, which I believe is the only one in the whole country. This is found in the west window of St Boniface Church, Bunbury. Together with Bunbury's patron and a Roman saint (possibly St George), Berteline, our local saint, is shown. He is kneeling with three stones in front of him which look suspiciously like loaves of bread, with his hands held up to Heaven.

There are two churches remaining with their dedication to St Bert and not Bartholomew. One of these is St Bertoline's at Barthomley, where the encounter with the Devil took place. It is said that the very stones from the miracle were once held in the church, but that was long ago, as they were missing by 1516. It is interesting to note, that this is also one of the sites where it is said the last wolf in England was killed in 1486. As its body was hung up, the blood from the creature's body dripped into the stream below and this became known as Wulvarn Brook. Coincidentally this is the spot where Bert stopped after he had lost his wife and child to wolves. The other church is in Runcorn, on Windmill Hill, where the dedication to Berteline is shared with St Christopher. And next to the church school stands St Berteline's Woods, which is said by local children to be the spot where Bert met the wolves. And so the folklore of St Bert remains and continues to be woven back into the landscape.

Seven

The Devil's Stony Features

The Devil gets blamed for everything. In Wales and Ireland it's giants, but in England we blame the Devil. So much of the landscape about Cheshire is said to have his fingerprints on it, and quite literally in some cases. We have a couple of names here for the troublemaker and both reflect the folklorish, gobliny character he seems to have acquired in many folk tales. One is Old Horny which, as well as bringing a wry smile to the face, does indicate that the Cheshire view of the Devil is one with the classic horned head. The other is the Urchin, which seems originally to have been a general term for goblin, but is also used in Cheshire for hedgehog. With these names in mind then, let us go back to a nebulous time to find out what Beelzebub (or is it Belcher Bob?) got up to in old Cheshire.

It probably started when the Devil was thrown out of Heaven. That troublesome Urchin tumbled from the sky and landed with a crash outside of Delamere Forest. He got up, all aching and throbbing, and rubbing himself over, and he reckoned that he was hungry. A great rumbling came echoing out of his stomach, and the Old Urchin realised that he was going to miss out on all the sumptuous food in Heaven. So he looked about, hoping to find something to eat down here on the Earth. And down by his feet he saw a worm wiggling. It had popped up thinking there was rain, but seeing how it was just the Devil bashing about, that wiggly worm decided better of it and started back down into the soil. But the Old Urchin saw a small snack and using his claws started to chase that worm. Digging after it, the Devil started throwing mud and stones and all sorts out of the earth, but the more he dug the more creepy-crawlies he came across. He popped the odd one in his mouth and crunched it with his teeth, but he wanted more, so he dug and dug and dug until he had dug out a long trench there in the earth. And there he was at the bottom, digging away some good few yards now from the surface, completely surrounded by bugs and beetles and worms and caterpillars. A veritable feast awaited that Old Urchin. And being the Devil he had the luck of the Devil. In all his digging and unearthing, he came across an old pan, perfect for cooking with. So down there in that trench, he made a fire and loaded up the pan with all those creepy-crawlies to make himself a fine buggy stew. It was such a rum concoction that a thick black smoke tumbled about the place, almost hiding the Devil, but he kept on digging and adding more bugs and such like to the gooey dish.

Now, there were some folk as were living nearby and they saw this thick black smoke coming up out of the ground, and they didn't need to think twice to know something bad was going on. So, a whole gang of them came over to where the Devil had been digging and stood at the edge of the trench looking down, wondering where the smoke was coming from. There was plenty of smoke, that was certain, but they could see little else. They could hear some scraping and a bit of a sniffing and, every so often, when the wind blew, they saw a brief view of some claws.

'It's a giant hedgehog,' said one of them, 'searching for bugs and the like.'

'What? Making a fire?' said another, not so convinced.

'Well, I as reckon it is an urchin alright, but a giant one.'

'What in these parts? I ne'er seen an urchin sniffling about here,' said another.

Well, soon enough they could all see what it was and they weren't best happy. There was a sudden big gust of wind and they could all see everything down there in the trench – the wings, the tail and the horns of the Devil himself.

'Ah, see it is an urchin!' said the first one.

'Aye, but not an urchin like you meant, it's the Old Urchin!'

And as soon as they realised that it was the Devil, they all grabbed hold of the stones which were scattered about and started to throw them at that enemy of humankind.

'Get yourself out of here!' they cried. 'We don't want you about the place, Old Horny, bringing your plagues and your lies!'

And with similar shouts they pelted the Old Urchin with a perpetual shower of stones. Well, whether he was the Devil or not, nobody would stay where they were being persecuted. So, shielding his head with his arms, the Devil flapped his wings and leapt up to fly out of his trench and over the heads of the folks. But that didn't stop them. They started throwing their stones up in the air, looking to knock Beelzebub out of the sky. The Devil could stand it no longer. He had only been trying to get something to eat when they started throwing stones at him. How would they like it? He decided to show them what it was like to be the object of such harsh target practice, and he was going to give them a really heavy lesson. The Devil had spotted a large stone, which had been uncovered by his earlier digging. Flipping himself over it, he cowered behind it to shield himself from the angry humans. Then, quickly digging further at its base with his long nails, the Urchin managed to get a good hand-hold on the enormous rock and lifted it up from the ground.

It took all his strength to get it up into the air, but it had the effect he had hoped for. The people soon realised what the Urchin was up to, as a great shadow fell across them. And they were about to run away as fast as they could. However, the Urchin was having a bit of a problem. The stone was so large and so heavy that he couldn't really control where he was flying with it. It was taking all his effort just to lift the thing and now he found he was shakily flying backwards, away from the people, and getting his toes caught in the uppermost branches of the trees. With each moment, Old Horny was losing out more and more to the weight of the stone and its awkward shape. He tried as hard as he could to keep it in the air and regain some control, but in the end he had to drop it. The stone plummeted to the ground, and landed with a reverberating thump between the villages of Peckforton and Tarporley. In utter frustration, the Devil sprung up on to that crag of a stone and leapt up and down. Shouting back to the people of Kelsall, he warned them that they may have escaped being flattened but he knew how to throw stones as good as any of them. He then jumped down to the ground where there was a large, round piece of granite. He climbed back on to the top of the stone, and so angry was he that he squeezed the granite in his hand. In fact, he made a shallow dent in the granite itself, in the shape of his thumb. However, the Urchin had more on his mind than patterns in stone. Winding up his arm, he took aim at the people over in Kelsall and threw the piece of granite through the air. Unfortunately for him, Eddisbury Hill was in

the way. The Devil was also pretty tired from his attempts to carry the big stone, so his aim may have been a bit off. The granite flew through the air only to hit the side of Eddisbury Hill and then rolled down to rest at the bottom with no damage done. A cry of laughter from the people of Kelsall rang out over the hills. The Devil knew he was beaten, for now. He leapt up off the stone and slowly flapped his wings, heading further south and vowing he would be back.

That stone, which the Devil had wanted to squash the folk of Kelsall with, is still there. It's a great crag which stands up proud in the Cheshire Plain, where the Sandstone Ridge dips down. It's known as Beeston Crag and is the location of Beeston Castle. And sometimes, when the mist rolls over the plain, it can look like that enormous stone has momentarily risen up from the ground. Maybe it is attempting to return to its first resting place outside Kelsall, but whatever magic allows that stone to rise up, it does not seem strong enough to allow the stone to leave Beeston. There it remains, giving a fine view of the Cheshire Plain to all who climb up to the castle, which is set on its highest point.

The piece of granite which the Devil threw at the people of Kelsall, at Urchin's Kitchen, is still there. It lies at the base of Eddisbury Hill with the shape of the Devil's thumb imprinted in its surface. It is known as the Devil's Thumbstone. But all this was just the beginning of the Devil's antics in Cheshire.

Eight

The Devil and Cheshire's Churches

When the Devil had recovered from that embarrassing escapade, he started to get up to his old tricks again, and it wasn't long before his target became the Church. All those churches about Cheshire, full of do-gooding folk, making a racket with their bell-ringing, he thought. Old Horny was determined to put a stop to all that. As he sat on Beeston Crag, he thought about his unfinished business with the people of Kelsall and, from that high point, Old Horny spotted the monks down Nantwich way who were building a church. With a leap and a flap of his wings, the Devil skipped over to the Peckforton Hills for a better look. Yes, there was a new church being put up at Acton. Well, he hadn't been able to throw a stone all the way to Kelsall, but maybe he could toss something over on those holy folk down there outside of Nantwich. Searching about, he came across a large enough stone – one which could cause a good bit of damage should it fall out of the sky. Then taking a more careful aim this time and with a heave-ho, the Urchin sent the stone hurtling through the air.

The monks of Acton were suddenly aware of something approaching them from the Heavens, and it was no angel.

They were about to run when they saw that whoever had thrown it either wasn't a good shot or had intended to miss them. The stone crashed into the earth about half a mile from where the building was taking place, so the monks continued with their work. But, both they and the local folk did talk about this stone coming down out of the blue. It soon became known as the Bluestone and it gave its name to the hamlet which came to be built there.

The Devil was furious. He could see that if this ineptitude continued then he would become a laughing stock and no one would worry about him or his influence on trouble in the world. He decided then to be more direct. With a flip and a flap into the air, he looked about for a completed church, one he could wreak some havoc on as an example to all the others. And there he saw it, St Chad's at Over.

As the Urchin headed off through the sky in the direction of Winsford, the monks saw his diabolical shape. Word quickly spread about his appearance, and they soon realised that it was the Devil who had thrown the stone, and that, therefore, he was trying to make trouble for the Church right across the land. So, when the Urchin reached St Chad's there were holy eyes looking out for him, watching him, ready to respond. The Devil had decided to try lifting something heavy again, as he had done with that enormous stone. He was fully recovered now and although his aim had been a bit off with the Bluestone, he reckoned that he could lift up a church, fly into the air with it and drop it down on to the Earth. Even if he couldn't drop it on those monks at Acton, the church crashing to the ground would smash spectacularly and that would be something for every Christian to remember.

So again, using his long, claw-like nails, he scratched and scraped about the foundations of the church until he managed to get it free from the ground. Then lifting one end, he clambered underneath, and, with a gargantuan effort, he pushed the building up off the earth.

All this time, a band of monks had been watching him. They had pretty much guessed what the Urchin was up to, but none of them was brave enough to take him on. They had another plan however, which they raced about with until all the monks of Vale Royal were in the know.

Just as the Devil flapped his wings to carry the church up into the sky, the signal was given. There was a sudden pealing of bells, which assaulted the air with its melodic clanging. The noise of the bells of all the churches of Vale Royal, plus the abbey itself, created a great wave of sound across the land, which battered the Devil's ears like an army of frying pans. He tried to fly up with the church, but he was torn between whether to let go of the church and cover his ears, or to grit his teeth and get as high as he could.

In the end, the Devil didn't get very high. The building was so heavy and the noise so loud that the church landed with a slight bump on to a small hill nearby. Initially, the Devil was trapped underneath, but as we know, he was a good digger and he soon burrowed his way out. It was an embarrassed and frustrated Devil who came up out of the ground there at Over, and all he wanted to do was get away from the gaze of the monks and plan his revenge. Of course, there was no way the monks could move St Chad's Church back to its original location and there it still stands, on that little hill outside of Winsford, to this day.

Nine

The Devil and the Monk

The Devil continued his assault on the Church in Cheshire with many other attempts to stop their building. He even turned his attention to the monks of Vale Royal Abbey, perhaps with the view of hitting the religious folk at their centre. The thing was that the monks at the Abbey seem to have been wilier than the Devil. The Devil therefore met his match when he tried to buy the soul of Friar Francis.

One night, as the monks of Vale Royal Abbey slept, the Devil came flying out over Delamere Forest. He knew a lot about these monks and was determined to not only disturb their sleep but also to take on their abbot, Friar Francis. Asleep in his cell, the abbot dreamt of pasties of fine venison and flagons of ale. How he wished such things would be the fare of every evening meal at the abbey. How happy his stomach would be and how soundly he would sleep. But suddenly his tasty dreaming was disturbed as he felt a sudden, sharp pain in his foot. Waking up he saw that sitting at the end of his bed, with a smile that glowed like the furnaces of Hell, was the Devil himself.

'Now then, abbot,' said the Devil, 'how would you like to be guaranteed your fill of pies and pasties and ale here at the abbey?

I know the things you dream of and I could easily arrange for such things to be brought to you … for a price.'

The friar was a little taken aback to see the Devil there in his cell, and for a moment thought about reaching for his cross to drive out the satanic visitor. But when he heard of the delights the Devil was offering and how there could be a constant supply, he decided to wait a moment and let Old Horny finish what he had to say.

The Devil clicked his fingers and suddenly, before the pair of them, a scroll appeared in the air. Without any hand touching it, the parchment unrolled and revealed a contract written in flame.

'See what is says here, Friar Francis,' hissed the Devil, 'I will provide you with all those delicacies you require, but when you die all those items which you own will be left to those who bury your body, and your soul will come to me.'

The abbot considered this. He did not want to sign his soul away to an eternity with the Devil, but a lifetime of good food was tempting. Friar Francis' eyes narrowed for a moment as he hatched a plan. Then suddenly his face was a picture of innocence with a sweet and cherub-like smile.

'Dear Devil, I will certainly allow you the care of my soul when I should die, but first let us be clear about what you will provide for me before that sad day arrives.'

'Very well,' said the Devil, thinking he had easily duped a foolish friar.

'Number one,' said Francis, 'Venison pasties every day. Number two, unlimited hogsheads of ale. And number three …' here his eyes narrowed briefly again, 'twelve tied bands of hay from Merton Sands. That's all.'

'Is that all?' laughed Old Horny, 'Pasties, ale and hay! How easily pleased you are!'

'I am an honest friar with simple needs,' bleated the abbot.

And so the two of them signed that infernal contract and off the Devil went to collect the three items named by the friar. The pasties and ale were not so hard, but the friar had been specific about the hay from Merton Sands. And so the Devil set off to find the grass, which would turn to hay. However, the Devil did not know that the men of Merton plough their fields so thoroughly every year that not a blade of grass is given the chance to grow. And even if a handful should make its way up, it would not be enough to create a dozen hay bands for the abbot. And so the Devil was kept busy by the cunning contract set by Friar Francis, not only in providing pasties and ale, but also by searching in vain for the grasses growing on Merton Sands.

Ten

The Dragon of Moston

For vast periods of its history, Cheshire has been a misty, boggy place. This wet landscape of meres and kettle holes has, of course, given rise to tales of all sorts of creatures living hidden in the murky depths, or concealed in the mist caught amongst the trees. And so tales of dragons slithering about in the shallow waters have lurked in the imagination of Cheshire folk, who had also heard tales of the ferocious dragons which populated the harsh mountains of Wales. The tales have been supported too by the discovery of some strange footprints found in the sandstone about the county. It seems that a creature now known as the *Chirotherium* did roam about the Cheshire Plain. It was not strictly a dinosaur, more of a large lizard, whose footprints show a thumb, making them appear more like a giant hand than a lizard's foot. It has been said that the possession of thumbs has given humans their advantage over the other creatures of the animal kingdom, but it seems like there could have been a challenger in the *Chirotherium*, whose name means 'thumb beast'. Did the cousins of this creature survive on in the watery world of our Cheshire Plain, and so create our own tales of dragons?

There was once a knight whose name was Sir Thomas Venables. He was a nobleman in residence at the family seat of Kinderton Hall. Late one afternoon, he was riding back from some campaign down a long road which would eventually lead to his home. The golden sun was shining on his armour and Sir Thomas was glad of heart. His campaign had been successful and now he was eagerly awaiting a warm bath in his home, but he had a few more miles to go yet. As the knight approached Bache Pool he decided it would be right to rest a while, for his horse had been ridden hard that day and the pool would provide the horse with the chance of a refreshing drink. Sir Thomas would also take the opportunity to sit in the sunlight, reflecting on the day's events. The pool stretched out on both sides of the road, which functioned much like a bridge in the way it traversed the watery expanse. It was here that the knight and horse stopped for a while as planned. However, it was as the afternoon edged closer to evening that the first threads of the Cheshire mist began to appear, hanging over the watery surface. They would soon cover the path and could very well make travel more treacherous, therefore Sir Thomas decided it was time to move on.

Now whilst the knight rested, a small boy – we shall call him Jack – had wandered down on to the very same path. He had simply walked out of the gate of his family's cottage, as a breeze had caused the simple lock to jolt, and the gate had swung open by itself. Seeing this, Jack had decided to walk out into the beckoning world and go for an adventure. No sooner had he stepped out, then the breeze blew and the gate swung back shut again, locking itself behind the boy. He wasn't worried. He was keen to see where his feet would take him and so his exploration led him down the path and on to the road, to where it passed between the waters of Bache Pool. Jack saw the great pool and hoped he might spy some fish there. And so now, just a hundred yards or so from where Sir Thomas was resting, a small boy stood on his own at the water's edge with no one to watch him. Although that was not entirely true, for a

pair of eyes was watching him. In the shadows cast by the trees on the distant bank, something saw the boy and slowly, ever so slowly, with only its eyes above the surface, it came sliding through the water. As Jack looked into the pool, he noticed all the little fish suddenly swimming away, and in turning to see where they were going, he looked away from the very reason for the fishes' departure. Closer and closer the watcher in the water came, rising up through the surface. Suddenly, through the mist came the long snout, fiery eyes, dagger-like teeth, snake-like neck and vast spreading wings of a dragon. That creature had the boy in its sights and stretched open its mouth to take him in one big gulp.

Hearing the splash of something rising from the water, and seeing the ripples bouncing across to where he and his horse stood, Sir Thomas knew something was wrong. He heard the cry of a child and suddenly could see, through the mist, the shiny bright-green skin of a dragon. Then he saw the foul creature's long neck, raising its head with a small boy in its jaws. The child's screams echoed out again across the water. The knight knew that he had no time to wait. In a moment, the dragon would throw back its head to allow its prey to fall into its mouth. The boy would be gulped down its throat and digested alive in the reptile's stomach. Like lightning, the knight of Cheshire reached for his bow and saw that he had only one arrow left in his quiver. He had no time to think of the severity of this moment, he simply aimed knowing that he had one shot only. As the string twanged, the arrow flew through the air, through the mist, and struck the dragon in the eye. Giving a roar, the dragon dropped the child and recoiled in pain. Sir Thomas knew it wouldn't be long before that monster recovered. If he did not continue his attack quickly, the dragon would be after the boy again. Sir Thomas leapt on to his horse, pulled her reins and, taking sword in hand, raced into the shallows of the pool, water splashing about him, and so distracted the dragon from pursuing the boy. Then, once he was beside the half-blind creature, he swung himself down into the water. Sir Thomas did not only carry a sword with him, he had a halberd, a dagger, a spear, a mace and many other weapons. He was a knight who was ready for anything. And so it was there in the shallows, with all those other weapons, that Sir Thomas manfully slew that beast, who only an instant before had been preparing to devour a child.

With the dragon dead, Sir Thomas turned to see Jack clapping his efforts with the excitement of a young child. It seemed that the boy was barely scratched; only his clothes were torn. As Sir Thomas was contemplating how he should find the boy's home, a cry came from down the road. It was Jack's mother, a widow with several children; she had needed to ensure that the others were looked after before she could set out to find her youngest. Now that she saw him, she came running down the road in floods of tears. Of course, when she saw the body of the dragon lying in the pool, its blood splattered on the rushes, and the knight standing there, she began to cry anew, realising just how desperate Jack's plight might have been. With thanks to the knight endlessly tumbling from her lips, the mother took her son in her arms. Amidst hugs and kisses and tales of what had happened, the two set off to return to their home, the mother swearing that she would never let Jack out of her sight again.

As peace returned to the lake and the mist continued to rise, Sir Thomas stood leaning against his horse, gazing at the body of the dragon. He then turned to reach into another of the bags he carried on the horse. He had many things with him, apart from his vast collection of weaponry. From one bag he produced a long, sturdy rope. After tying it about the dragon with good strong knots, he returned to his horse and attached the ends of the rope to his trusted steed. Then, slowly, the knight made his way home, sitting in the saddle whilst gently encouraging his horse to continue forward, dragging the body of a dragon behind her, after an already exhausting day.

When Sir Thomas reached Kinderton Hall, the servants all rushed out of the house to see the fearsome beast slain by their master. Sir Thomas gave orders for the body of the creature to be nailed up on the large barn door, where it could be displayed for all who passed that way. And the knight would ensure that there would be someone on hand to tell his story.

Many years later, when the body of the dragon had rotted and many of the bones had been lost, a depiction of the beast was painted upon the barn door. And many more years later, when the wood of that door had rotted and needed replacing, it was decided that an image of the dragon with the boy in its jaws should be painted on a shield. Hanging over the door of Kinderton Hall, this became the coat of arms for the Venables family. And now, in the church of Middlewich, named St Michael and All Angels, there is a chapel in memory of the Venables family, and here there is a shield which bears the image of the dragon as painted on that shield at Kinderton Hall. It stands as a record of the adventure which Sir Thomas Venables met all that time ago at Bache Pool, along the road that is now known as Dragon Lane.

Eleven

The Runcorn Dragon

The people of Runcorn – or Rumcoven as it used to be known – lived in the shadow of the more illustrious abodes of Norton Priory and Halton Castle; one a place for men of God, the other a place for men at arms.

Now, it so happened that one night a farmer was dozing in front of the fire in his farmhouse, exhausted after a hard day's work. His wife, meanwhile, was no less tired but had many other things to do before she could rest and so was busy. Suddenly, the door to the house jolted. It was locked, but it sounded as if something had been thrown against the door with force – something large. The farmer still slept, but the wife turned to look at the door and wondered what could have happened. Then it jolted again and she dropped the plate she was holding. The crash awoke her husband with a start, but she told him to hush and beckoned him over with a shaking hand. Confused, he got up and staggered over to her, still not fully awake, and she hastily whispered that she thought someone was trying to get into the house. He then decided to see what was up, but not to open the door. He crept up to it, with his wife following close behind, and then opened the little flap in the top of the door, which let him see who was there without letting them in. His wife peered over his shoulder. Scared as she was, she was also intrigued by the situation and who it could be that was causing such trouble so late at night. The moon was shining, but they could see very little because of what appeared to be mist. But they could smell that it wasn't mist. There was the reek of brimstone – was something on fire? As they peered out, the smoke cleared a little and there on the pathway lay something white. It was a dead sheep, its side pierced by what looked to have been five spears – or so the wounds suggested. And the blood from these wounds not only stained the wool black, but was streaked along the path to the very door itself. As if the poor creature had been dragged from the front door and left to lie there.

'That must've been what was thrown at the door just now,' surmised the wife, 'one of our sheep! Who would do such a thing?'

But then there was a roar and something far bigger crashed down in front of the door; its sudden appearance made the farmer stumble backwards, almost knocking his wife to the ground. He returned to the door flap and saw a great scaly creature standing on the path, licking the blood of the sheep. Its dark scales caught the moonlight and its long thin claws sliced through the animal's flesh as the monster feasted. The farmer and his wife did not stop much longer. Instead, they turned and ran out of the back of the house, through the fields and over the hill to the next farm, where, once they had got their breath and drunk some ale, they recounted what had happened.

News of this creature spread about the villages rapidly. Some said a dragon had come and others called it a demon. Whatever it was, sheep started to disappear from the farms in the area, as well as the odd cow. Parents feared for their children, and all who lived in the area were afraid to go out at night, but they were also wary about staying home. Many sleepless nights were had, with people sitting in the kitchen all night with a pikel or club in hand.

There was in Runcorn, at the time, one particular blacksmith. He was a man of no nonsense, who knew his work and did it well. He too had heard of the demon-dragon and many who came to have their horses shod would speak with him about it, all shaking their heads saying, 'What are we to do? What are we to do?'

'We?' he would say, 'We? I don't know about you and I, when there's others that can deal with this,' as he continued to strike the iron on the anvil. 'What about those knights up at the castle. They're supposed to be the Constables of Cheshire and I work ensuring their armour's all it should be. Let them prove their worth and slay the dragon as knights are said to do.'

'But what if it's a demon?' responded his customer, 'Sword and armour's no good against spiritual forces.'

'Well then,' he answered as he turned to the forge, 'there's the friars up at the priory. I've done many a job fixing them up with crosses and alike. It's time they used one of them to exorcise the accursed creature.' He turned to eye his customer, 'Nope. We're working men, you and I. We've got enough to get on with just making sure our families are fed. Let them who live in fine castles and divine retreats start to earn their keep.'

And with that he returned to his work, believing he had more to worry about than someone's missing sheep.

However, the blacksmith was about to find that the demon-dragon would very well be his own problem. It was only a few nights later, when the blacksmith was rudely awakened by the most terrible racket coming from his cowshed. He had never heard old Ruby making so much noise and so he went tumbling out of the house to see what was going on. There was such a commotion in that shed that he just knew she wasn't in there alone. Just for a second, he thought that there could've been a bull in there trying to give his old Ruby a reminder of the old days, but then he saw the roof of the shed bowing as if whatever was inside was trying to push its way up and out.

'It's that demon-dragon thing,' he breathed, 'trying to steal my old Ruby. Well, we'll see about that …' And he turned tail to run to the forge and grab his largest hammer. Then, sprinting back to the cowshed, he shouted, 'You leave my old Ruby alone.'

But before he reached the gate, the roof split open and two leathery black wings burst out, pulling up the black scaly body of the demon-dragon, which was carrying in its claws the blacksmith's old cow. Up, up, up they went, from the cowshed and out across the fields.

'No you don't!' shouted the blacksmith and gave chase. As the demon-dragon flew over the hill, the blacksmith followed, cursing the beast and demanding the return of his property.

The demon-dragon paid no attention to the shouts of the angry man, but continued to flap through the air with the cow, which was decidedly heavier than a sheep. This meant that the blacksmith was able to keep up and follow quite easily, so that when they eventually came to Windmill Hill, he saw the dragon land in amongst the woods atop that mound.

As he pushed his way into the bracken, he could hear the mooing of old Ruby and following the sound, he soon found her abandoned in brambles. Perhaps she had been too heavy for the demon-dragon and that creature had crashed somewhere else. However, as the blacksmith leant over to check his prized cow, a flash of fire caught his eye and he could here a hubbub rising up from not so far away.

'What in name of Belcher Bob ...?' he wandered over through the trees to the place where the flames leapt up, and the sound of strange voices seemed to be coming. And when he arrived at a clearing of trees, he was amazed to see he was standing on the edge of a pit; a pit which contained not only the demon-dragon, but a whole host of ugly creatures, all of which seemed to be climbing up out of a hole in the bottom of the pit. A hole from which flames were rising and an evil stench of brimstone filled the air.

'Hell's bells,' gasped the blacksmith, 'I don't remember seeing this pit afore, but this looks to be dug reet down to the underworld itself and all sorts of demonic things are tumbling out.'

The blacksmith realised that if no one stopped them, these bogeys and hobgoblins would take over the land. He lifted the

enormous hammer above his head and raced down the sides of the pit, roaring with all his might. Kicking and hitting as many of the satanic brood as he could, he beat them soundly to stop them making it any further up the sides of the pit. God forbid that any should escape! That blacksmith's hammer came crashing down on many a head, buffeted many a stomach, cracked many a back and crushed several dangly parts as he fought to stop every single one of them.

There was so much noise and such a bright light from the flames that, very soon, the men of Runcorn appeared. Gawping, they stopped around the top of the pit in disbelief at what they could see and who should be doing it.

'Don't stand there like men of clay,' shouted the blacksmith as he hit a rather toothy goblin in the mouth, 'we've gotta stop this lot from getting out. I've beaten a few back down, but we gotta plug up this hole! Start filling the pit in quick!'

Then the men all rushed off to get spades and picks and buckets and whatever else they could find. Then, as the blacksmith continued to bash and smash the demonic horde, the men dug and threw the earth down into the pit.

As the clay-rich soil began to fill up the hole, so the blacksmith stood on the growing pile of earth, using his boots to push the odd bogey back down, adding a good knock on the head to be sure. Until finally, as the cock crowed on one of the farms, it could be seen that that hole was well and truly plugged, and there was not a hobgoblin or demon-dragon to be seen.

And the men were so in awe of how the blacksmith had valianly fought such creatures that they wanted to lift him up on their shoulders and carry him back into Runcorn as with a hero of old. But, even though he needed to rest, he managed to stand and say, 'Nay, don't be silly now. I am only a working man looking after his own. I don't want accolades or pointless parades. Let's just say job done and leave it at that. And now ...' he said, looking about, 'where's that old Ruby of mine? I left her somewhere here abouts and she wasn't looking in a good state.' And off he went to find that cow of his, whose abduction had made him into a hero.

News of the blacksmith of Runcorn soon reached the ears of the Constables of Cheshire up at Halton Castle, and the ears of the friars of Norton Priory. However, both groups of learned men were embarrassed to hear of how a simple working man had saved his people and his land from such diabolical dangers. They therefore agreed that it was probably an exaggerated tale, and one which would not be worth writing down. And so it was left for ordinary folk to remember, which meant that it became the domain of children and storytellers alike.

Many years later, when the story of the blacksmith had all but been forgotten, the pit was dug out by the marlers, who were after its clay-rich soil. If you go up on to Windmill Hill you will see the crater-like landscape left by those gangs of men, and one of them is the pit which almost released a host of hellish fiends on to the earth. If you should be up there, take a look and see that there are no cracks or wisps of smoke coming out, because if there are, you'll need to quickly find a blacksmith who is handy with his hammer.

Twelve

Sir Gawain in Cheshire

Like many parts of the country, Cheshire claims that King Arthur passed through. There is the whisper of a story, telling of how, when King Arthur was on the run from the Saxons, he hid in the burnt-out remains of that Celtic hillfort up on Maiden Castle. However, the most famous tale from the Arthurian canon must be that of 'Sir Gawain and the Green Knight'. Although we do not know who the author was, the great work of poetry looks to have been set on the Cheshire borders. The English in which it was written makes good use of the local dialect, and it's incredible that there are still people today, 600 years later, using many of the words contained in the original narrative. Despite its great age, the story was only discovered about 200 years ago, and so was hidden from the likes of Alexander Pope and Dr Samuel Johnson, who, no doubt, would have had something to say and so would have influenced our modern view. The tale has had some attention, most famously that of J.R.R. Tolkien and more recently the poet, Simon Armitage. Throughout, the hunt has been on to establish where exactly the locations mentioned in the tale are to be found in the United Kingdom. With its origins in that mysterious part of the country where Staffordshire,

Derbyshire and Cheshire meet, all three counties have made a claim on the poem, professing they have the site of the castle of Hautdesert and the Green Chapel. Many scholarly attempts have been made to justify these claims and, indeed, the Wirral Peninsula is mentioned by name. My retelling, of course, follows the local belief that Sir Gawain did, in fact, face his greatest challenge here in Cheshire. However, the original is too beautiful and clever to be handled effectively in prose, and so you must read that for yourself. My version then takes some liberties with the story, which I hope will help to present this adventure to the modern reader.

***

And so it was that Gawain, a young knight of the Round Table and nephew of King Arthur himself, came riding on his steed, Gringolet. A long and hard journey it had been but still Sir Gawain continued, for he had a knight's errand to fulfil. In just one week, after almost one year of searching, he had to find the elusive Green Chapel. The young man had experienced many adventures already, and now he was wet and freezing in his armour. His journeys had taken him along harsh rocky paths through the deep valleys of Wales. He had seen mountains rising up on either side of him and continued through wind and hail to make his way further north. Finally, the sun had shone as the Irish Sea appeared before him, its light glinting with hope, but little heat, off the rolling waves. Of course, his road had not been without obstacles. There had been bears and wolves. And then those fearsome wild men, the Wodwos, who would hang about in the shadows of rocky outcrops, hoping to catch a lone traveller unawares. With sword and shield and skill he had overcome all attacks, but despite his regular victories, little by little the hope in his heart was being chipped away.

So, when Phoebus' light showed across the vastness of the sea again, it was with welcome eyes that the sight was received. Renewed a little, Sir Gawain and Gringolet galloped along the sand with the salt waves splashing up, until they came to Holyhead. And it was there that Providence seemed to be on their side, for the waters of the Dee estuary were low and both knight and steed could ford their way across to the wild peninsula of the Wirral – a place known to the Welsh as Cilgwri, and one known as the dwelling of a wild people who have long been forsaken by God. For Thomas Hughes tells us in his Werall Hundred that 'this was in old time a Forrest, I think I cannot be doubted; but when it was disafforested I will not contend, only that it is now one of the most fertile parts in the whole County.' Alas, Gawain was not in the times of Thomas Hughes, and so our knight chose to avoid the thick darkness of the forested land, knowing that it would only lead him to the coast again. He therefore turned southward and wandered on to a smooth land of fields. Here he spurred on his horse and together again the two raced, but this time across the Cheshire Plain, leaping cleanly over any wall or hedgerow that blocked their way. It was as if they were hunting an invisible quarry or seeking to outpace an unseen opponent.

Soon the open fields turned to woodland and Gawain's pace was quickly reduced. Entering the wooded lands, the ground itself became wet and soft. Gringolet's feet squelched and slipped, mud splashing up to add another covering of dirt to the once shining armour on both horse and rider. They passed menacing black-watered meres and took care not to slip into open-mouthed marl pits; soon Sir Gawain had to dismount and lighten the load on the struggling stallion. Taking the reins in hand, the young knight pushed through the thick mud, leading his horse step by step, until he could bear it no longer. He crashed down to sit on a log, holding his head in his hands, whilst the horse stood attentive. Its breath joined the surrounding mist which floated about them; its ears turned this way and that, catching sounds inaudible to the hapless knight. It was there, alone in Delamere Forest, that Gawain's mind rolled back the months to recall the very event which had brought him on this search.

Thoughts of the fire that raged in the great hall of Camelot flickered in his mind. Memories of good cheer resounded in his head, as he recalled the Great Hall on New Year's Eve with his fellow knights, as they continued their celebrations of Christmastide. Sir Gawain had been sitting beside his queen, Guinevere, who was in turn beside her husband, the famed King Arthur. And together they had overseen the festivities of their merry tribe – the knights and their ladies. Suddenly, a cold wind had skitted across the floor as the two great doors were flung open by an unknown knight, who came riding into the royal presence. Armoured in green, he sat proud on his horse which he steered across the floor – its hooves clipping on the stone. The horse too was dressed in verdant raiment, and it seemed in the light that the hair of its supple body was also of the same colour. The strange knight pulled up his steed defiantly before the king himself. Any one of those knights would have risen up and pulled the rider from his horse, incensed that he should be so insolent as to not dismount before the king, but none moved. For the knight was not even a member of the human race it seemed. His armour and horse were not the only things which were green; the skin of the knight himself was this colour too, but of a deeper shade. He rode without a helmet and so all could see his head, which looked even larger due to his unkempt locks, wild like a thicket. And from wide green lips came a deep booming voice, which echoed around the hushed gathering.

'Arthur, King of the Britons and Knights of the Round Table, I come here this New Year's Eve to issue you, men of renown, with a fearsome challenge.'

Here the Green Knight raised a sprig of holly above his head in a sign of peace – the leaves as dark as his own skin, but the berries bright as an echo of blood. Yet in his other hand, the challenger brandished a stick with a harsher prick, for there he held an axe. Its handle was long and thick like the branch of a tree, and its head heavy with a green blade that glinted in the light, catching the shimmers of the Great Hall's fire.

'Which of you will take this axe, step up here and swing the blade to meet my neck? For whichever of you does this to me, will then allow me to do the same to him one year hence.'

The Green Knight's voice echoed about the hall but no one answered, or even allowed themselves a breath. Even though a swing of the axe may kill the insolent cur, each knight thought, this fellow appears so unnatural that it may be that he will not so easily be killed …

'I'll do it,' came a voice, 'I will take your challenge.'

Stepping out from the royal table came the king's own young nephew, Gawain. In his mind, he surmised that if he should hit the Green Knight well with the axe then his head should be lopped off the shoulders, and there would be no way that the monster would return in a year's time.

'Ah ha,' laughed the giant who now slid down from his horse, 'so it is the youngest from amongst you. Come forward then, Little Hawk, and take the axe, if you can indeed carry it.'

The axe was heavy but Gawain was not weak. And as he adjusted his hold, the Green Knight prepared himself. Leaning forward, his long locks reaching to the ground, the knight cleared all stray hairs with his hand to expose his neck. Then, summoning his strength, Sir Gawain lifted and swung that blade through the air. It whistled as it arched and fell clean on to that greenish neck. The combined strength of the young knight and gravity saw the blade slice cleanly through flesh and bone, like a knife through Cheshire cheese (a green cheese). And as the head fell to the floor and bounced, so the axe rang out as it hit the stone floor and stuck into it. A cheer leapt up from the knights and joyous Gawain wrestled the axe from its chink in the stone to raise it like Excalibur, a young man again victorious in Britain. And as the feet of knights twitched, itching to kick the head of that menacing gatecrasher like a hairy football, they stopped and silence reigned again; for they were all frozen, as movement came from where it should not. The decapitated body rose, chest and shoulder lifted up, and hands reached forward. Then each foot stepped to follow the guiding hands, which searched, fingers spread, for that member of the body which had been separated from the whole. Crouching down, two five-legged spiders raced across the floor, fumbling at table legs and warriors' feet until they found the head. Then grasping its hair, the head was lifted up and swung for a moment like a pendulum, turning slightly with each swing, until it stopped. Then the great green lips moved again, as the eyes opened to view the terrified assembly.

'Where is Gawain, that brave young man?' The head asked, 'Step forward and hear your instructions.'

Allowing the axe to drop to his side, Sir Gawain stepped round to be addressed by the severed head.

'On this day, one year from now, you must meet me at the Green Chapel, and there your neck will meet the axe, as was the bargain that was made. Ask about for the Green Knight and the Green Chapel and you will find me. You have one year, what more time do you need!'

And with those final words, the knight turned, still with his head hanging from one hand. He clambered up to his horse and, taking the axe from Sir Gawain, turned about and rode from the hall, the doors closing by some mysterious force behind him.

With the hall still in silence, Gawain looked at the floor and the pool of blood, red as the berries from the sprig of holly, which lay on the stone also. He had severed the head from the shoulders of that Green Knight, the blood was proof, and in one year hence it would be his turn.

***

Now, Gawain was on this hunt. Yet, with all his travelling, he was still not certain how close or how far he might be from that chapel of the Green Knight. How much longer did he have to search in the cold and the wet? He shivered again in the chilling metal which surrounded his body. If only there was a place that he could stay – to be warm, to be fed, to have company. And in his desperation, he rose to his feet and cried out to Our Lady. But the only answer he received, it seemed, were tiny white flakes falling from a grey-pink sky. This was not the weather to remain sitting still. Sir Gawain again took the reins of his horse and led Gringolet to some semblance of a path, to find a way out of that forest.

As they walked, watching the gradually growing carpet of white around them, Gawain looked up through a gap in the trees and saw a hill. Atop that hill there seemed to be a dwelling, a dark shape that, as the sun for one moment broke through the snowy clouds, was shown to be a mighty castle – a place to stay. Renewed in strength, Sir Gawain leapt back on to his horse and headed through the forest to where the castle stood. It was called Hautdesert, but was known to the local people as Eddisbury.

It was here that Gawain received a warm welcome. The lord of the castle, Sir Bertilak, welcomed the young knight with open arms. His embrace almost crushed the weakened Gawain, so strong was the knight – a mighty warrior and a mighty huntsman. The servants took away the visitor's armour for cleaning and repair. His horse was led by the groom to the stables to be watered, brushed down and bedded with fresh straw. And Gawain was given fresh clothing and food. It was over this sumptuous meal that he related to his host the tale of his adventures and the reason for his quest.

'Why!' laughed Bertilak with thunderous tones, 'The Green Chapel is but a handful of miles from here. You must stay and then, on New Year's Day, I will send one of my men with you to guide you to the place. But for now, rest here, enjoy our hospitality and celebrate the Christmastide with us.'

And so, this was how Gawain found himself in a bed – his head resting on a goose-feather pillow and his body warmed by sheets and furs. But, as his mind mused on these thoughts, and as he turned to sleep again, he heard the sound of fumbling at the door; a click as the handle was turned and the slight squeak of the hinge. Then the soft delicate padding of footsteps not wanting to be heard, making their way closer to the bed. To be ready for what would happen next, but knowing that he was expected to be asleep, he turned his head to one side and kept an eyelid lifted slightly, so as to see who was coming to his bed.

A bright light shone into the canopied space as one curtain was pulled back, and there, standing in the light, was the lady of the house. As if she was feeling the sides of her beloved horse, she slid a hand on to the bed. With one easy movement she slipped into the space to sit on the bedside. Then lifting her feet, she swung her legs up and around so that now she was on the bed itself. Dressed in a long white shift with golden trim, her arms exposed and her hair trailing over her shoulders, the light shone through where she had entered, highlighting each curve of the beauty she possessed. She then crawled towards the supposed sleeping knight, and, lifting her dress a little, positioned herself so that her thighs were either side of his blanketed legs.

'Sir Gawain,' she whispered enticingly, 'Oh, Sir Gawain, will you not awake?'

Of course, Sir Gawain had been aware of every movement and watched what he could from the now tense angle of his head under a flickering eyelid. He could pretend no longer, so faking a yawn he turned to face Sir Bertilak's lady, twisting his body, with legs gently trapped underneath her own.

The lady giggled and lifted herself slightly to allow Sir Gawain to turn, and in doing so raised herself towards his waist a little more, her head lowering and her lips coming closer, for a second, to his own.

'Do I not bring a beautiful beginning to your day, young knight?'

'Why yes, my lady, I cannot imagine a more beautiful sight to greet one in the morning. But where is Sir Bertilak?' Sir Gawain knew full well, as the two had discussed the elder knight's plans the night before.

'He is out hunting and will be gone all day …' And the lady's voice trailed away, as she lifted her head and gazed about her, considering what on earth the two of them could do with so long a time before them.

'Maybe we could … talk,' suggested Gawain. He recalled how on announcing his plan to go hunting that morning, Sir Bertilak had not only told Gawain to remain in bed and rest, but also said that they would have a little game. When he returned from his day in the field, Bertilak would present the young knight with whatever he had won from the day. And whatever Gawain won, he should present that to Bertilak – an exchange.

Here now was the prettiest woman Gawain had seen – save for Guinevere maybe – and she was sat upon him in the bed and keen to suggest some pursuits the two of them might engage in. If Gawain was to succumb then what would be the result of their endeavours? In winning the lady, what then would he have to present to Sir Bertilak? In his mind he knew that he could not betray his host and yet this woman smelt so sweet and was full of attention for him.

'What should we talk of?' she asked, a little surprised at his suggestion.

'I am a Knight of the Round Table,' he replied, more as a reminder to himself and his resolve, than as a subject for small talk. However, he thought it might work. 'Yes, there are many knights in the service of King Arthur and each one has performed a feat of chivalry to gain a seat in the lauded position.'

'The lauded position?' she laughed with a knowing glance, 'You must show me that.'

'A place at the Round Table,' continued Gawain hastily. And so he went on to name each one of the knights, as best he could remember them. And for each he did remember, he would recall their exploits, telling of how their acts of bravery had brought them great renown. But some of the names were difficult to recollect, and he confused some of their adventures. He was distracted somewhat by the way her ladyship leant forward appearing to listen, but instead took her slender finger and dallied between a playful stroking of his hair and a tracing of the shape of his ear. Until finally, he could not utter the name of any further knight and said with sudden resolve, 'Mass!'

The lady moved back, slightly surprised, 'Mass?'

'Yes, I must take morning Mass. If your ladyship will excuse me, I must arise.'

'Arise? I thought you had already risen,' she said with a wry smile.

Ignoring her suggestion, Gawain repeated his need to take Mass that morning; he truly knew within that he must be cleansed that day. And so the lady made to slide off the bed, but just as she returned to the open curtain, she stopped and turned back.

'I must admit, Sir Knight, that I am a slight bit surprised. You are a knight of renown and although your host's lady has shown you much attention, you have not once offered the politeness of greeting her with a …' she licked her lips slightly with the very tip of her tongue, '… a kiss.'

Suddenly, Sir Gawain was hot with embarrassment. He did not wish to offend her ladyship, but he was not sure that such an act was entirely necessary. Still, it may mean that she moved on and he could get to Mass.

'I sincerely beg your pardon, my lady. I did not mean to insult you. Please give me a kiss if you so wish …'

'I do,' she answered immediately and leant within the body of the bed to place her lips to his. The sweet smell of honeysuckle rose up in his nostrils and filled his blood. He could feel the softness of her cheek brush against his. And then she withdrew.

'One will be enough … for today,' she whispered. Then she slithered away from the boy and disappeared through the curtains to finally leave his bedchamber.

Mass was said with much fervency by Sir Gawain that morning, down in the chapel of Eddisbury Castle, or should I say, Hautdesert. And he then managed to avoid meeting his ladyship again until the late afternoon when, to both his relief and apprehension, Sir Bertilak returned home.

'Ah, Sir Gawain,' he called, fresh from a day out in the open, 'you are looking well after your morning of rest. There is a life in your eyes and more energy in your step, young knight. And so, allow me then to present you with your prize.'

Gawain was about to correct his host – not only was the prize more truly Sir Bertilak's but also, remembering their agreement, he knew that he would have to return the favour. Yet, before the young knight could protest, Bertilak called his men forward and they presented Gawain with the prepared flesh of a wild boar. The conquered beast had been skinned, sliced and now was served on a platter before him. Sir Gawain gulped thinking of what his fate may have been had he allowed himself to be conquered.

'And did you win anything this day?' asked the hunter lord.

'Indeed,' answered Gawain, who then stepped forward and kissed his lord full on the lips, the master's red beard prickling his chin.

Sir Bertilak was a little taken aback at first but then he laughed, 'So, you have done well today, Sir Gawain. And how did you manage to win such a prize? And from whom I wonder?'

'Ah now, my lord,' the young knight answered, 'Our agreement was to exchange those things we gained in our day. There was no mention of revealing details and so I will not say.'

''Tis true,' laughed the host again, 'Let us then prepare for our evening feast and enjoy more of your company, handsome knight.'

'And let us feast on this boar, my lord. You have given me this fine flesh and therefore I choose to share it with my host.'

And so they did. With song and stories and much laughter, the household enjoyed the spoils of that day's hunt. Many hours later, as the final embers in the fire of the Great Hall finally turned from red to grey, the castle fell silent but for the snores of all those who had feasted well.

Over the next two days, Sir Gawain was left to sleep in his bed each morning as Sir Bertilak and his company thundered through Delamere Forest on their hunts. Each day, the lord was successful and so returned one day with a deer and the next with the remains of a fox. But, what of Sir Gawain? What prizes did he win on those days and so exchange with Sir Bertilak?

Again, on the first morning of these two days, the lady came to visit him. Again, her body slid in close to that of the young knight. Her soft voice and gentle touch were there for him to enjoy, but only behind the curtains of that bed. But Sir Gawain found strength again to resist, and still received a kiss only, which was followed by a second, on that day. And so it was that the deer from Sir Bertilak's hunt was exchanged for two kisses from knight to knight. And again, Sir Gawain felt the prick of the older knight's beard.

On the following morning, much the same situation took place amid the bed sheets. Only this time, upon Gawain's refusal, the lady stopped and slowly undid her cloak. As her slender hands untied the kirtle bound about her willowy waist, Gawain wondered if he could maintain his resolve even if this undoing was leading to a fuller view of his ladyship's offerings. However, it was the kirtle itself she was to offer.

Sliding the soft green satin through her fingers and slowly placing it about the young man's neck, she told him that this was a magical kirtle. It would turn away any blade raised against him. She wanted him to have it, protection against any sharp assault. And once she had given him this favour, she pressed her lips to his three times – a kiss for each of her morning visits.

When it came to late afternoon, as the winter sun was falling behind the horizon and the sound of hounds came echoing into the castle, Sir Gawain now wondered on the agreed pact with Sir Bertilak. Until this day, he had always given his host that which he had received. These were only kisses. However, as the lady had presented Sir Gawain with the green kirtle, he had been reminded of the true reason for his presence in this castle. He was on his way to face the Green Knight, that great and terrible figure who would soon take a swing at his neck with the heavy, sharp axe. The thought of that dreaded day had lain dormant in the young knight's mind as he enjoyed the comforts of a Christmastide at Eddisbury. With the reminder had come a solution. If what her ladyship had said was true, then this green kirtle would ensure that his head remained on his shoulders. Yet there was the agreement made with Sir Bertilak. If he should hold on to the kirtle then he would be dishonouring his host. If he should give the kirtle to his host, then he would again be facing certain death.

Sir Bertilak strode into the castle hall, his face red with the efforts of the day's hunt.

'Ah, Sir Gawain,' he bellowed, with a slight loss of breath, 'here is what I have for you this day.' And he held aloft the bright bushy tail of a fox.

'And here is what I have for you,' said Sir Gawain, stepping forward and giving his host three kisses, his face again brushing against the bristly beard.

'Three kisses,' laughed Sir Bertilak, 'And no more?'

Gawain wondered what he could mean. Did the knight refer to the kirtle? Did he know? Could he tell Gawain was hiding something? Or was he referring to the kisses? Was it that three was more than he had expected and he was jesting with the young knight?

Then Sir Bertilak laughed again, 'It is perhaps good that tomorrow you must leave for your quest at the Green Chapel, for who knows how many kisses I should receive as each day passed!'

Gawain laughed too and the pair of them walked out of the castle hall, Sir Bertilak regaling his guest with the details of that day's hunt.

Yet all the time, Gawain's heart sank. He had withheld something from such a generous and good-hearted host. And he knew that tomorrow the real reason for his presence in this county would sharply rise before him.

It was the morning of New Year's Eve. The frost hung on the trees that lined the path down from Eddisbury Hill back towards Delamere Forest, and again Sir Gawain shivered in his armour. He was wrapped in a thick fur cloak, a gift from his host, but still he trembled. Ahead of him and Gringolet, a servant from the castle led the young knight, riding on a pony. Occasionally he turned back, partly to check that Gawain was following, but also to observe his constitution.

'Good Sir Knight,' the servant ventured, 'the cold darkness of this forest will soon pass and we will enter the meadows of the Ruler of Elves. Know then that the site we approach is less cast in shadow. The view is in fact quite pleasant there, Sir.'

'Indeed?' Gawain whispered through chattering teeth.

'If I may be so bold,' continued the servant, 'I observe that you are somewhat uncertain over this encounter you must face.' The servant could tell he was scared, but trying not to show it. 'If you should want to take a different path … say, one which would return you to Camelot? Then know, Sir, that I would not tell. You may leave this quest now and none would know.'

Gawain heard the man's words, his offer. The thick forest about them did not help to quell his rising fear. The silence and stillness down that frozen path seemed to only increase the sound of his beating heart. But Gawain had already held on to the green kirtle and so dishonoured his host. If he was to now break the pact made with the Green Knight, then his keeping of the kirtle would be for nothing. The kirtle was now wrapped around his neck, hidden under his tunic, beneath his breastplate and all concealed by his cloak. If he was to leave now, then he would dishonour two knights. How could he return to Camelot carrying in his heart two such breaches of chivalry?

'I will complete the task,' he replied with as much conviction as he could muster, and his voice echoed down the path ahead of them from frozen trunk to frosted stone.

As the sound faded into the dense forest, they arrived at the meadows of the Ruler of Elves, the place now known as Alvanley. Out from the forest and across the open fields, the servant indicated the rest of the way for Sir Gawain, saying that he must leave him, for the knight must face his fate alone.

After watching the servant ride back on his pony along the path, lost from sight in the darkness of the overhanging trees, Gawain then turned to see where he must go. And there before him stood a great snowy cat, tall and proud with strength resting in its shoulders. It was as if the creature had appeared to remind the knight of what there was in his own self, deeper within than that fear which fluttered through his mind. And so Sir Gawain dismounted and approached the beast. It showed him where he might drink and he took courage from the White Lion.

Refreshed and renewed, Sir Gawain ensured he had his sword and shield, brushed the snow from the fur of Bertilak's cloak and began the walk up to where the Green Chapel lay. Along the path, lined with red sandstone, he strode resolutely, but with each step he could hear a sound rasping along the stone walls. It was the scraping of metal on a whetstone – the sharpening of an axe. He grasped his sword a little tighter and moved on, passing the walls of sandstone, or was it stained stone? Blood-stained stone? Until, he turned the corner to see the Green Knight. With his hair like the bushes of the forest, dressed in his verdant armour, standing taller than Gawain remembered from that night one year ago, that Green Knight held the axe in one hand, but there was no sprig of holly in the other – no sign of peace. There was no redness of the berries about the knight on this day.

Both knew what was expected and, with silent indication, the Green Knight showed where Gawain should kneel. With the removal of his helmet, the placing down of his sword, shield and cloak, Sir Gawain knelt before the giant warrior, praying that no sign of the green kirtle would be evident, and that it would protect him as promised.

Then, stepping forward, the Green Knight swung back the axe and the blade flashed through the freezing air, a cloud of vapour surrounding that fearsome face as he released a breath. And as the axe fell towards the young knight's neck, Sir Gawain flinched. A moment's fear overcame him and he pulled back from the axe's path.

There was a clang as the blade hit the stony floor and the Green Knight stared at Sir Gawain.

'You moved,' he growled, 'do not recoil. Remember your honour, young knight.'

Gawain nodded and prepared himself again. And so the axe was wielded high a second time, and came flashing down. But this time, it was the Green Knight who caused the axe to miss. Sir Gawain stayed still as directed, but the Green Knight had not held the handle correctly and so the swing was misguided.

'Stay,' he growled again, 'our pact is that the blade should meet your neck. I will try again.'

And so, his knees against the stony ground, his body trembling in the cold with no cloak to protect him, Sir Gawain hoped to God that the kirtle would prove true. With his eyes now closed, he heard the grunt of the Green Knight as he heaved up the axe, the whistle of it cutting through the air and then a sudden pain in his neck. Yet he was still alive.

Gawain opened his eyes and reached up to the exposed flesh. Pulling his hand back he saw there was blood, but his head remained upon his shoulders. Leaping to his feet, he grabbed helmet, sword and shield. Fitting them back on with fumbled haste, he stood, armed and ready to face the Green Knight in whatever fight might now ensue.

But from that severe and determined jade-like face, a laugh rang out, a laugh which Sir Gawain thought he recognised. And then the Green Knight began to shift into another shape. The colour of his skin drained away, the roughness of his hair and the greatness of his stature, all transformed until, standing before Sir Gawain, was his host of Christmastide, Sir Bertilak.

Flummoxed, the young knight pushed up the visor to better view this wonder, and asked in halting questions what had happened, and which of the men was the true self of this figure before him.

'Ha, I am Sir Bertilak and this is my true self,' revealed the now red-bearded man before Sir Gawain. 'All this, my young knight has been a test, a trial for your honour, being a Knight of the Round Table. You have been tried and although you are a man of chivalry, there is a thread of cowardice about you.'

And before Sir Gawain could ask more or step back, Sir Bertilak strode towards him, lifted his helmet, and searched with his fingers beneath the neck of the breastplate, before extracting her ladyship's green kirtle. Red were Gawain's cheeks now as he realised that his hosts had been in cahoots all through his stay. He knew that his actions, the attempts to protect his own life, did not fit with the code of chivalry and not with the contract made with Sir Bertilak.

'Sir Gawain,' continued the host, seeing the young knight's downcast face, 'You kept this kirtle for yourself believing it would protect you when, in truth, you should have passed it to me. However, who can blame a man for wanting to protect his own life? Sure, your contract with me was breached, but other men would have made much the same choice. Be of good cheer, young knight, for you have proved yourself worthy in many other areas. You came this day when you had the opportunity to go. And you resisted the charms of her ladyship on three occasions, passing on to me all the kisses you had received from her. I therefore allowed you to duck from the axe on my first swing, in recognition of the chasteness of your character. I then allowed the axe to miss you on the second swing in recognition of your honour in being here this day. And the third swing? I did indeed ensure that the axe met your neck as promised back in Camelot, but only a nick to your neck.

This wound is there as a reminder of how you did not come to me in full, pure chivalry, but you live because there is more knighthood about you than not, and you should live to continue on the virtuous path.'

Gawain was pleased that he should live, but a shame hung over him for his selfish choice.

'Stand tall, young knight,' encouraged Sir Bertilak, slapping Gawain on the shoulder, 'you have done better than many others would. And now, return with me to Eddisbury Castle, where we may celebrate and see the coming of the New Year. Morgana le Fay would be pleased to see you again, now that you know that all that has passed was simply a test.'

Gawain was suddenly taken aback. 'Morgana le Fay?' he repeated.

'Yes, of course, King Arthur's half-sister, your aunt. It was she that charmed me so that I could take on the shape of the Green Knight and she appeared as my lady at the castle.'

'My aunt?' breathed Sir Gawain, recalling images of that lady sliding through the curtains on to his bed, the closeness of her body and lips, the sweet smell of her skin and what could have happened if he had not be so strong in his resistance. 'With my aunt!' he gasped again.

'Come, a roaring fire awaits and Morgana is looking forward to welcoming you back,' urged Sir Bertilak.

'I thank you, indeed,' Sir Gawain hastily replied, 'but I think it best that I return to Camelot now. The pact has been fulfilled and I am sure I am wanted there, if only to tell my tale. Give my regards to Morgana le Fay and I will pass yours and hers on to my king.'

Then, briskly, Sir Gawain turned about, retracing his steps along the path to meet his horse Gringolet. And climbing up to begin his journey back to Camelot, he thought of all that had passed in those recent days. Of how he had faced death and temptation, and all that could have happened, and what might have happened as a result of weakness. He had passed the test, but he was uncertain over his true knighthood.

Leaving Cheshire, he rode towards the south, following the marches in the west to find his way back to his king. But still his mind returned to what might have happened. What if he had fallen for Morgana's charms, the beauty of his aunty? And what would he have been duty-bound to give Sir Bertilak, his uncle? He decided that he should not dwell on such things, but focus on the future battles he may have to face. After all, there are some thoughts that can make you lose your head.

Thirteen

The Wizard of Alderley Edge

This is the tale at the beginning of Alan Garner's book, *The Weirdstone of Brisingamen*, and the series which follows it. His books celebrate the wealth of tales contained in this fascinating landscape, as well as drawing on many other ancient influences.

This is a tale from ages past which has left its mark on the countryside, and again links to King Arthur.

They say that on one morning in 1697, a farmer was travelling from Mobberley to Macclesfield through the mist on a milk-white mare. He was sitting high, confident of the fine price he would fetch at the market for this steed. However, as the two approached that place known as Thieves Hole, the horse stopped. The farmer was surprised at the sudden break in their journey and looked ahead to see what had caused the animal to halt. There, in a dip in the road, the morning mist had thickly gathered, but a breeze floated over and the soft white screen wavered to reveal a man with a trailing beard, looking as if it was part of the mist itself. He wore a long cloak with a beaten, pointed hat and carried a twisted staff.

'Let me buy that mare from you,' the old man called out.

'Oh no,' called back the farmer, 'I'm off to the market where I'm bound to make a good price for this mare. I'll be beating off all those making me an offer so I'm not gonna settle for a price now and miss out on the big one.'

'Let me tell you then,' said the old man, his voice wafting along the road like the breeze about them, 'you will not be able to sell this mare at the market and I will meet you again on this road when you return home.'

The farmer didn't know what to make of this odd fellow's words, but he had met strange folk many times before and knew that often it was quite safe to ignore their ramblings.

'We'll soon see. We'll soon see,' said the farmer, who saw the old man step to one side as his horse began trotting forward again.

Down at the market everyone agreed that this was the finest milk-white mare they had ever seen. In fact, a crowd gathered about to see the creature for themselves. Yet, even with the hubbub and the great numbers coming to view the horse, not a single person made an offer. The farmer could not believe the lack of interest and as the day waned, he came to realise that the words of the strange old man at Thieves Hole were in fact the truth.

Riding back home along that road from Macclesfield to Mobberley, the farmer was not happy. He was wondering if the old man had put some sort of curse on him or told folk not to make an offer. And so, when they arrived again at Thieves Hole, passing through the evening mist, the horse stopped again, and the farmer had a word or two to say to the old man. A breeze floated over the path and the mist in the hollow parted to reveal the hat, cloak, stick and beard of the mysterious fellow.

'Now then,' called out the farmer, 'what exactly have you been up to? This mare of mine should have fetched me a handsome price but none made me an offer. It was just as you said and I am not best pleased.'

The old man did not volunteer any explanation, he only said, 'Then I will buy her from you and you will not be displeased at the price I shall pay.'

Then the old man stepped back, beckoning for the farmer to follow him. Only the farmer did not have much choice. His horse was off as soon as the old man turned, plodding up the road and tailing him on a baffling trek.

As the sun slowly sunk down behind Alderley Edge, the old man led the farmer and his horse off the road and down a path. Together they passed Seven Firs and Goldenstone. The farmer was so concerned about where they were going and what would happen that he did not look about him, but then he would not have seen much as it was getting darker all about. However, if he had looked about his surroundings, he would have seen images of the elderly man who was leading them down unfamiliar paths. A carving of his face had been etched into a rock nearby and underneath stood a stone trough, collecting fresh water from out of the ground. On this rock there was, and still is, the inscription which reads as follows:

Drink of this and take thy fill, for the water falls by the Wizard's Will.

Together the three went on to Stormy Point. Then past Saddleboll until they could go no further, for their path was blocked by a great smooth rock. Then, before the farmer could ask what was going on, the old man lifted his staff to point at the rock. The sound of thunder rolled over their heads without warning and the farmer grasped the reins of the mare more tightly. The smooth rockface before them cracked down the middle, splitting open to reveal a pair of iron gates. And beyond the gates there was a tunnel lit with flaming torches set in the walls. Despite the farmer's hesitancy, the horse continued and followed the old man through the gates and into the tunnel, the clopping of her hooves echoing about them.

After some minutes, the tunnel opened out into a great chamber, a cave which resembled the crypt of a cathedral. Set throughout the cave were two long lines of stone plinths, and, on each, a man in armour did lie. Beside each of these stood a milk-white mare, each looking as if they were waiting patiently for the knight beside them to awaken from his momentary rest. There was, however, one plinth bearing a knight which did not have a horse standing beside it. The old man then looked at the farmer and reached for the reins. 'You will be well paid,' he said.

And so the farmer clambered down from his horse, too awestruck to argue. He watched as his mare was led by the old man down the row of sleeping knights to arrive at the place where one more horse was needed, completing the waiting cavalry.

The old man then returned to the farmer as he had promised payment, good payment, to this man.

'This is why I needed your horse,' the wizard explained, 'Each knight is now fitted with a steed. All are ready should the great and terrible day come.'

'What day's that?' asked the farmer, still not sure about what was happening.

'The day when Britain is in direst peril. For on that day, King Arthur will rise together with his knights. And they will ride out from this place, each upon a milk-white mare. And in their purity, they will stand against the enemy, driving him and all his forces out of England and into the sea.'

There wasn't much the farmer could say to answer that, so he resorted back to what he knew, 'You said something about being well paid?'

The old man nodded and led the farmer to an opening in the wall of the vast chamber. Here there was another cave, a little smaller, but piled high with sacks. The sacks were so full that their contents had spilt out on to the floor. The farmer looked.

'Salt,' he said, 'Is this whole cave full of sacks of salt?'

The old man nodded.

'And that's it?'

The old man nodded again.

Well, the farmer knew he could get a good price for salt and there was a lot of it here.

'Take whatever you can manage,' offered the old man.

It wasn't money, but the farmer was happy to take what he could. In fact, there was a handcart hidden amongst the sacks and with that the farmer took a great deal of salt.

Finally, with the cart loaded, the wizard escorted the farmer back up the tunnel, through the gates and past the split rocks to join the path again. Then, as he pushed the cart up over the rock pathway and into the night, the farmer heard a sudden clap of thunder. Looking back he saw the rocks had rejoined. There was simply one smooth stone blocking the way into that enchanted cave.

Under the moonlit sky, the farmer headed home as quickly as he could. It wasn't easy in the dark, over the bumps and dips and with such a heavily laden handcart, but in the end he made it back to his farmhouse. His wife had initially thought that he had sold the mare for such a good price that he had been spending some of the money down at the pub, but as time had gone on, she had become a little worried. A man wandering home, a bit worse for wear, carrying a large amount of money, on his own … he could have been robbed. But when she saw the handcart, and heard his incredible tale, she had very little to say, other than, 'Did you check to see whether it was really salt?'

'Huh!' coughed the farmer, 'I saw it there in the cave with my own eyes.'

'Did you now?' she said, peering into one of the sacks, 'And what do you think this is then?' And from out of the bag she pulled not a handful of salt, but a handful of diamonds.

The farmer had thought he'd seen everything that day and almost keeled over. But instead, he dived on to the sacks and opened every single one. There was not a grain of salt left in any of them. Instead there were diamonds, rubies, emeralds and sapphires.

'Well, well, well,' laughed the farmer, 'that old wizard fellow said I'd be well paid. Well paid! We'll never have to work again with all this. To think that I wanted to sell my horse at the market!'

And he was right, the farmer and his wife never had need to sell horses, cattle, sheep or chickens again. Although, they did keep the farm going, as idle hands are the Devil's tools. And that milk-white mare still waits deep in the chamber behind the smooth rock at Saddleboll, waiting for that evil day which has not yet come. And when it does, we know that the farmer's horse will be there, with the army that will ride out to drive Britain's enemies away into the sea.

Fourteen

Robin Hood's Tump

Roger Lancelyn Green, the author and collector of myths and legends, lived at Poulton Hall on the Wirral, which is something of a fairy-tale place itself. To begin with, the Hall has the chilling tale of a wicked old squire, who trapped a young nun in one of its rooms for his own evil purposes. Both their spirits are said to still reside in the house. On a more charming note, however, the gardens are full of sculptures and settings relating to *Alice's Adventures in Wonderland*. These features aside, Green is most well known for the many collections of folk tales and fairytales which he retold over several decades. In *The Adventures of Robin Hood*, Green takes two of the most important tales in the hooded man's canon and places them in Cheshire, without losing the link to Sherwood Forest. In retelling 'The Lytell Geste of Robin Hood', Green makes the most of the knight in this story being Sir Richard of Legh, by reminding the reader that Sir Richard's family seat is High Legh, which is found in Cheshire. He then goes on with the iconic tale of the contest for the fabled Silver Arrow. Set in Kingslea Park (Kingsley near Frodsham), Robin Hood takes on both the archers of the Forest of Delamere and those of the Forest of the Wirral. Sir Richard is referred to as the Hereditary High Forester of these two regions. The bowmen of Cheshire put up a good show against the outlaw, being renowned throughout Europe for their skill. In fact, our Cheshire archers would often form the artillery of the English armies in the battles on the Continent, being feared for their devastating storm of arrows. But, in this particular contest, it was the man from Nottinghamshire who was victorious. Robin's enemies, however, were not going to let the outlaw get away. As Sir Guy of Gisbourne attempted an arrest, Sir Richard provided sanctuary to Robin and the Merry Men. In doing so, he made enemies of Sir Guy, the Sheriff of Nottingham, and Prince John. Green goes on to tell how Robin Hood promised his host, 'We will together to Chester, there to beg the aid of Earl Ranulph.' Now, it was Sir Ranulph who oversaw the building of Beeston Castle, drawing on the design of castles he had seen in the Holy Land. At this point, we leave Roger Lancelyn Green's retelling and return to some local folklore.

It is said that Robin Hood did arrive at Beeston Castle, but when he got there the guards did not believe who he was, and so would not take him to Sir Ranulph. Robin asked them what proof they required, and so, after some conferring and a scratch of their heads, the guards decided that if this really was Robin Hood then they should make the most of the opportunity and see some fine archery. They took him to the top of Beeston Crag and showed him a small barrow in the distance, some 2 miles away. They said that if he was really Robin Hood, then he could prove it by firing an arrow from the castle down to hit the barrow, dead centre. Robin looked, rolled his shoulder, wiggled his fingers and felt the wind. Then he took an arrow from his quiver, placed it in the bow and pulled back the string. He eyed the distant mound and then aimed up into the air. Letting go the string, the arrow whizzed up into the sky. Its path then bent and down came the tiny missile to land dead centre on the barrow. The soldiers gasped and then cheered. With hearty slaps to Robin's back and shaking their heads in wonder, the soldiers could not believe their luck to have met the famous hooded man and they gladly took him to the Earl of Chester. And that barrow, an old burial mound at Tilstone Fearnall, still remains. The arrow has long gone, but it is thought to have been used as a practice target for the local bowmen in the days of Edward III, and such mounds were known as butts or tumps. However, because of that incident at Beeston Castle, this particular mound now has the name of Robin Hood's Tump and you can still see it on Vale Road off the A51.

According to Green, Robin did manage to convince Sir Ranulph, Earl of Chester, to back Sir Richard of Legh. And together they marched on the residence of the Sheriff of Nottingham, putting both him and Sir Guy of Gisbourne back in their place.

Fifteen

SIGHTINGS OF DICK TURPIN

As every part of England likes to make claim to the heroes and villains of our national legends, so it's said that Dick Turpin passed through Cheshire a number of times. He is said to have raced through on Black Bess at some record speeds, but he still managed to stop off at three of our inns.

The first of these was an attempt at an alibi at Hoo Green. Dick had just robbed a lawyer at New Bridge Hollow on the Chester road, outside of Altrincham. In the scuffle, the highwayman's pistol had gone off and the lawyer was killed. Determined not to have this murder attached to all the crimes already listed against him, Dick Turpin leapt on Black Bess and they tore off down the Chester Road. After about 4 miles or so, at breakneck speed, Dick arrived at the Kilton Inn. An ostler was just coming out to see to one of the horses, when, without any provocation, Dick rode up to the lad, leant over and slapped him across the face with the handle of his riding whip. Then, as the ostler stumbled back, Turpin asked him what the time was. Once he had an answer, the highwayman said, 'Know then, sonny Jim, that it's Dick Turpin that asked you this.' He then jumped down from his horse and handed Bess over to the very same ostler.

Looking about, Dick saw a small group of gentlemen enjoying a game of bowls nearby. He walked over the road to join them and to simply watch the game, whilst making sure they told him what the time was. Then he turned back to the inn to refresh himself after that afternoon's hard riding. I daresay Turpin enjoyed his flagon that night, knowing what was to happen.

When the authorities eventually caught up with Turpin, he of course had an alibi and plenty of witnesses to verify it. At the time that it was said the murder took place, the ostler was able to confirm that the rogue had not been in Altrincham, but at the Kilton Inn throwing his weight around. The gentlemen who liked a game of bowls could also confirm this. And it was felt that there was no way anyone could have committed a murder in Altrincham and then be at Hoo Green in such a short space of time. Dick was therefore allowed to go free.

This wasn't Turpin's only foray into Cheshire, as there are two other pubs which make a claim to the highwayman. One is the Hawk Inn at Haslington, where the locals say Dick stayed with Black Bess, the horse being made comfortable in the stables. Soon some constables arrived looking for Turpin who, being tipped off, leapt out of the upstairs rear window into the stable yard. Then he was up on Bess, and as the authorities came out through the back door of the inn, Dick rode towards the closed gates. In one leap, Black Bess rose over the gates and almost cleared them clean. Her hind leg just clipped the wood, but horse and rider still made good their escape. The pub remains but the gates are no longer there.

The other pub making claim to the scoundrel is at Warburton, where a less dramatic, but equally intriguing, escape is said to have taken place. The Saracen's Head is a fascinating establishment, which hosts souling once a year and holds a relic from one of the Knights Templar. With all this, it is also said that the inn was a hiding place for Dick Turpin, who would use an underground tunnel to quickly disappear if any constable got wind of his presence. The tunnel is still talked about, but its location and entrance seem to have been lost.

And finally, the locals around Millfields, Nantwich, talk about how Dick Turpin stopped over to sleep in a place known as Hawkes Cottage, which once stood on the corner of Marsh Lane and Dig Lane. Sadly, the building was demolished in the late twentieth century, but photos of it do exist. Some say it was a barn and others talk about how it was once a pub known as The Raven. Was Turpin taking lodgings in the pub or was he simply hiding in a barn? Either way, the mark of Dick Turpin has been clearly left right across the county of Cheshire and the hooves of Black Bess have clattered over our roads, fast and furious.

Sixteen

A Fiennes Lady on a White Horse

When people ask me where I live, I constantly have to reiterate that I live in Bunbury in Cheshire, and not Banbury in Oxfordshire. It may be due to there not being another Bunbury in the whole country. Although, it sounds such a typically English village name that you expect there to be several about. The mistake may be due to people being more familiar with Banbury, having seen it signposted off the well-travelled M40. And, of course, Banbury is better known, being featured in a nursery rhyme:

> Ride a cock-horse to Banbury Cross,
> To see a fine lady upon a white horse;
> With rings on her fingers and bells on her toes,
> She shall have music wherever she goes.

There are many versions of this rhyme, but it is said that the second line originally read, 'To see a Fiennes Lady upon a white horse.' Many have forgotten the intrepid Lady Celia Fiennes, and so it seemed to make more sense to say 'a fine lady'. Yet, Lady Fiennes made a quite remarkable trip around Britain in the seventeenth century, riding side-saddle on a white horse, and there are tales of her journey through Cheshire, which provided her with a rather unique experience.

Lady Fiennes was the sister of William Fiennes, who was the 3rd Viscount of Broughton Castle in Banbury, and so the town gained its association with this strong-willed woman, as in the nursery rhyme. She set out in 1682 to ride around the country, often only accompanied by two servants, and wrote a journal chronicling what she saw and the adventures she had. She would have had to travel along some pretty unkempt roads and through some dangerous landscape. It was on her travels through Cheshire that the whole enterprise could have ended, and would have done so in quite a grisly fashion.

On part of her 'Great Journey', Celia and her two servants travelled through Christleton, where she is now featured on one of their stained-glass windows. She also came to the Hockenhull Platts outside Tarvin. These old bridges were built for packhorses to be able to cross the River Gowy, and the marshy lands around its banks. There have been bridges here since Roman times, and Celia Fiennes seems to have wanted to cross on the bridges like all those who had in times before her. She recorded how wet the area was then, referring to 3 miles of causeways through woodland and how she passed several large pools of water. Celia was also surprised to not see as many cattle as she had expected. She knew of Cheshire's dairy farming and its cheese, but said she only saw between twenty or thirty cows in any herd that she came across. On asking the locals, she found that one village would make its cheese using the milk of all the surrounding farms. Such combining of resources meant the milk would go further and so produce the great cheeses for which Cheshire was famous.

Lady Fiennes then continued to follow the Old Coach Road from Chester towards Tarporley, where she then joined the older mediaeval route, turning more directly southward towards Whitchurch in Shropshire. The road from here became noticeably rougher and completely deserted. The sharp form of Beeston Crag rose up against the flat landscape as the small party rode away from the township of Tarporley and into some more wet and wooded areas. It was as they were passing through the shadows of such a place that two rather surly types came out from the trees some distance behind them. Looking back, Celia and her servants all agreed that the two men who were on foot looked as if they had something hidden under their coats – maybe firearms. Quickening their pace slightly, but not wanting to create suspicion, the three travellers moved on, hoping to reach somewhere more populated very soon. The footpads – for that is what they were thought to be (roadside robbers who travel on foot rather than on horseback) – continued following, maintaining their determined pace. Over the next few miles, with each turn in the road, the party of three hoped that they had lost the menacing pair, but always they appeared from around the bend, continuing their unassuming pursuit. The road took Celia down past Brown Knowl and No Man's Heath, before Whitchurch finally came into sight. Fortunately for Celia and her two servants, it was market day in the town and very soon the road became more populated with people travelling back and forth. It was at this point that the two dubious characters disappeared – probably thinking they had missed their opportunity and now was not the time.

This seems to be the only time that Lady Celia Fiennes encountered any form of trouble on the road in the whole of her trip around the country, and this was in Cheshire. There now stands in No Man's Heath a sculpture by Jeff Aldridge, which was commissioned to mark the 300th anniversary of the Fiennes lady's passing through the village. It is situated on the corner of Old Coach Road and Back Lane and although it's officially called the Celia Fiennes Waymark, locals refer to it as The Monument. It is claimed to be the only permanent monument to the memory of Celia's journey, but we do also have the aforementioned stained-glass window at Christleton. Therefore whilst Cheshire provided a more threatening experience for Lady Fiennes, we have also ensured that her journey is well remembered here.

Lady Celia Fiennes must have been quite an exception in her time – a woman going on such a dangerous journey during the seventeenth century. And some of those genes for exploration and adventure must be a marker of the Fiennes family, as Sir Ranulph Fiennes continues her tradition of pushing against expectations to make great personal achievements.

Seventeen

Old Nell and Other Bears

For a few hundred years here in Cheshire, bears were a common feature of people's day-to-day lives, and there are many indicators of this found about the county. The village of Burwardsley is said to have once been 'bearwardsley,' meaning the meadow of the bear-keeper. There is a mysterious cave at Broxton Hall which, as well as a tiled floor, a window and a door, has some intriguing scratches in the wall, resembling those that a bear might make with its claws. A large stone by the church at Audlem is said to have been the place where a bear was chained up to perform for the villagers. And so these bears, which were taken around the county, became a major feature of the Wakes in each town and village. The Wakes were an annual celebration, occuring on the parish's saint's day. The day would be full of an array of entertainments and events, such as pudding eating, tobacco smoking and hot tea drinking. In Audlem, the first man to get drunk that day would win the title of Mayor. With the Wakes being so widespread and happening on different days throughout the year, a bearward could find himself having a fairly regular income, if he got his bear to the next town or village. For generations, the bear's part in the festivities would be a bloody fight against the locals' fiercest dogs: bear-baiting. In later years, this was replaced by the more genteel dancing bear. It is said that one bear, known as Old Nell, regularly visited the Bunbury Wakes for fifteen years. I am not sure if she was the same Old Nell who was housed at Middlewich, some 14 miles away, but both Old Nells seem to have shown a liking for ale. In Bunbury, there's tell of how she would saunter off after her turn of bear-baiting at The Square and visit the Nag's Head pub, at that time an establishment in Higher Bunbury. There she would have a bowl of ale and settle down to sleep in the shippon round the back of the hostelry, until all the festivities were over. The bearward would always know where to collect his charge, and, having had a drink and a sleep, she would merrily follow him off to the next location.

Whilst in Middlewich, Old Nell would follow her bearward off to the local Red Cow to share a beer with him there. It seems that the two had such a good understanding that the bear was able to help her warden out of a spot of bother. Having got himself into arrears on some payments, he soon found his possessions seized by the local constable. With Old Nell in tow, the bearward went down to see if he could talk the constable round. Knocking at the door of his house, he placed Old Nell in the doorway ready to greet the constable. As the door was opened, the bearward called out that he thought the fellow looked lonely and could do with some company. Dutifully, Old Nell growled and the constable fled back into the house and escaped by climbing up and out of the chimney. With the constable out of the way for a while, the bearward loaded his things on to a bogie and headed off home, followed by his faithful bear.

In 1883, all bear-related events across the country were finally banned. However, there were rumours of secret bear-baiting going on in the depths of Delamere Forest. The ban was both in recognition of the cruelty to the bear and the danger to the public. An example of such hazards is the fate of the bearward at Barthomley. It is said that he was

rent to pieces by his own bear and so a ban was placed on all such entertainments in that village. This wasn't simply an abolition on bear-baiting in Barthomley, but an end to all the festivities associated with the Wakes. It seems that these local celebrations could easily get out of hand in many of their activities and were often berated from the pulpit.

Eighteen

The Congleton Bear

The most famous bear of Cheshire must be that of Congleton. The bear has become so synonymous with the place that Congleton is also known by the name of Beartown. The Congleton Wakes were a major event on the town's calendar, as they were for almost every village and town, and, of course, as with all the others, the main highlight was the bear. Every year, the people would talk about the coming Wakes, and the bear. They would discuss which dogs would be taking on the beast and what their chances would be. As each day passed and the Wakes drew nearer and nearer, the excitement grew. Children couldn't sleep, and bets were taken at the local inns. However, it was on the very night before the Wakes themselves that the bearward burst into the pub in tears. Many guessed straight away what had happened, but they couldn't bring themselves to speak it out. With bated breath, the whole pub waited until the bearward had downed his beer, recovered his faculties and announced, 'Our dear old bear – has died!'

A gasp rose up from the crowd and a sadness dissolved all the previous merriment. No one could imagine the Wakes without a bear. All the years of pleasure that bear had brought them, and now she was gone. It was a difficult moment for all there that evening. On the one hand they needed to grieve over the loss of such a popular figure in the town. On the other hand, the Wakes were the following day and they needed a bear. But, where would they find a replacement at such late notice?

Now, there was a slimy fellow who lived in Congleton who was always able to get hold of whatever a person might need, as long as you didn't ask too many questions. He was sat at the back of the pub sucking on his pipe listening to the discussions, until he called out, 'You know, I could get y'all a bear.'

Everyone stopped talking and looked at the little man. Ah yes, they thought, if anyone could get a bear, it would be him. But they all knew what he would say next.

'But it'll cost yer.'

The slimy fellow named his price but none knew how they could find the kind of money he was after at such little notice. Others said it was ridiculous to ask such a thing. Didn't this chap realise the importance of a bear to the local community? Didn't he have a heart? Some got quite shirty over his request for such a payment, but he did point out that a bear can last for up to fifteen years and they ought to see this as a long-term investment.

Discussions continued and various deals were attempted between the folk in that pub that night, but nothing seemed to be working out. They still needed to find the money.

So, then the slimy fellow made another suggestion. He knew that the town had been giving a lot of money to the church recently. The church Bible was gradually falling to pieces and they really needed a new one. As with bears, Bibles don't come cheap but once you have one, a good one, it will serve you for a good number of years.

''Ow about the money you've been raising for the new church Bible?' called out the slimy fellow, 'Could the church make do with the old Bible for a little bit longer?'

There was even greater consternation now. Which was more important – a new church Bible or a new bear for the Wakes? It was eventually decided that they should ask the vicar, and they all ought to buy him a drink, after all, he had done a lot for the people of Congleton. They would buy him a drink or two and just put the idea to him.

A small gang of men went up to the church and found the vicar preparing his sermon notes, which happened to be addressing the indulgent ways of the Wakes. His plan was to launch into a tirade against such irresponsible behaviour on the morning after, when everyone would have a sore head and already be thinking that they'd made a few mistakes. However, he was very surprised at the gents who appeared, full of praises for his work and saying thank you, to show their gratitude. He felt he really couldn't refuse and said he would join them for one quick drink. And then it was another. And then another.

As the vicar sat there at the bar, generously supplied with a constant supply of ale, he noticed that the whole pub seemed to be watching him. Was he really that popular?

'So vicar,' ventured one of the men who had brought him in, 'your flock is in great need and requires some assistance.'

The vicar, who was in quite a contented mood now, asked how he could help. The man then went on to explain how the bear had died and how such a creature was the highpoint of the Wakes, which was the highpoint of the year for the community. And how there was a large collection of money waiting to be spent. Initially, the vicar was not happy with the idea. He did not like the Wakes as it was, but to take that money, the money collected and set aside to purchase a Bible, and spend it on such a thing as a bear? He could not allow that to happen. But after a few more beers, he started to be more open to the idea. A few more, he was able to say that perhaps he could loan some of the money. And finally, even though he could hardly string the words together, he agreed that the money was there for the people to use as long as news of this did not go further than the parish.

Overjoyed, that gang of men hoisted the vicar on to their shoulders and marched him down to the safe where the money was kept. The pub emptied as a late-night parade followed the now so popular man-of-the-cloth. A new, younger bear was bought and what a bear! The tussles with the dogs were faster, more thrilling. The people cheered and clapped and many said the slimy fellow wasn't so bad after all.

However, the morning after the Wakes, when the vicar had recovered from his hangover and all had sobered up, a guilty congregation entered the church. With sore heads, they watched the vicar very carefully attempt to turn the pages of the Bible so that they did not flutter off with the slightest breeze. And because he had not attended the Wakes, but taken the day off to recover, he was in full voice and vigour to let those people know how irresponsible and ungodly those Wakes were.

Despite the vicar's caveat in the pub, word spread telling of the people of Congleton, who had taken the money collected to buy a new Bible and spent it all on a new bear. The town was, for a while, a laughing stock and became a place for many to measure their piety by. For whatever misdemeanours other people had got up to in life, none of them had ever taken church money to buy a bear.

Nineteen

The Smiling Warrior

This particular bear comes from more modern times and even though he did not set foot in Cheshire, he was a local legend for a short while. This was thanks to the Polish Resettlement Corps camps, which were set up all over the north-west of England and North Wales. For Cheshire, these were in Oulton Park, Vale Royal, Pettypool, Blakemere Hall and Delamere Park. It was whilst the Polish armies were receiving training in Iran, that some of the soldiers from the 22nd Artillery Supply Company were working up in the mountains. They heard an unusual sound, like a deep, throaty mewing. Following the noise, they stumbled upon an abandoned bear cub. The mother bear was nowhere to be seen and the soldiers were unable to leave the cub behind. It would have died out there alone, so picking it up, the men brought the bear cub back to camp with them. The other soldiers were thrilled to have a bear brought into their camp. It certainly brightened up the monotony of their training. And so the company adopted the bear as their mascot. Calling him Wojtek (pronounced voy-tek), meaning the 'smiling warrior', he quickly became the most popular member of their Company. He was fed on condensed milk and initially slept in a washing-up bowl. Of course, he soon grew too big for this, but continued to sleep with the soliders in their tents.

As Polish soldiers came to the camps in Cheshire, stories of Wojtek quickly spread about the place. The soldiers' families soon arrived in Cheshire too and, naturally, military fathers were pleased to tell their children of this amazing bear. They recounted how, when the Company was due to leave Iran for Italy, they could not face leaving Wojtek behind. He was therefore drafted into the Company. His own documentation was drawn up and Wojtek became the first official bear soldier. It was at the Battle of Monte Cassino, in Italy, that Wojtek really showed his worth as a solider. He helped the men by loading ammunition, and being stronger than any of the other soldiers. Wojtek could carry more boxes. He therefore helped speed up the supplies reaching the front, which may have given the Poles the edge. Films and photographs of the soldier bear started to circulate amongst the Polish troops, and many turned up at Delamere Park. There were pictures and stories of how Wojtek would drink beer, like Old Nell before him, as well as smoke cigarettes. There were, of course, friendly wrestling matches with the soldiers.

Once the war was over, Wojtek was given a home at Edinburgh Zoo. He lived there until he died in 1964, but had become a legend all about the country. Not least in Cheshire, where a curious relationship with bears has been part of our history, with tales from the Polish soldiers only adding to the bear mythology of the county.

Twenty

The Witches of Cheshire

Throughout history, older women who lived alone, either by choice or through necessity, were often ostracised by society and in times past were even suspected of being witches. It could be that simple eccentricities, such as keeping a pet eagle in a shed, could bring the accusation. This was the case with the witch of Burwardsley, who also, fittingly, lived near a place called the Witch Pit. An old woman, living on her own, keeping an eagle and living near the Witch Pit – has to be something strange doesn't there … and so it goes on.

Since those days, the Witch Pit has been filled in and yet, people still talk about hearing strange noises emanating from the place at night. Others keep a store of salt by the fire, in case a suspected witch passes by; they could then throw a handful into the flames and so ward off any magical influence. There was also a great suspicion of toads. If one was found to have wandered into a house, then the wisdom was to catch the amphibian and immediately throw it into the fire. The fear was that this was a witch in the guise of a toad. The toad was often a shape they would supposedly take on to sneak into someone's house and eavesdrop, learning secrets, which they would then use to their advantage. The witch-toad could also gather tiny fragments of the house owner, such as fallen hairs or nail clippings, and these could be used in forming curses against them.

Delamere Forest is one place which is also supposed to be full of the dark arts, despite it being invaded each weekend by the dog walkers, cyclists and high-wire climbers. Many of these tales stem back to the idea of the fabled Chamber in the Forest. There are whispers that there was once a castle in the forest, which fell into ruin. As the plants began to grow between the bricks and find their way into the gaps and cracks, the remains of the castle were slowly hidden from the view of most people. It is then said that the witches of the area found it and liked its obscured location. Down in the cellars of that old fortification they would meet; a secret gathering place for their coven, where they could practise their arts without disturbance. And so, the name of the Chamber in the Forest took on a menacing feel, when the truth is that the construction was more functional than magical.

It is true that a fortification was built, but this was not amongst the trees of the forest. In the building of her defences against the Vikings, Ethelfleda, the Lady of the Mercians, reinforced the old hillfort atop Eddisbury Hill to become one of her line of burhs. However, years later, in 1337, Edward the Black Knight ordered the construction of a new chamber on the side of the hill, that would serve as a hunting lodge. The site provided a good view over the forest and was on the main east-west route through Cheshire, which followed the old Roman road of Watling Street. This was when it became known as the Chamber in the Forest, and was a base for the Royal Foresters. However, as routes across the county changed and the old road was abandoned, it was no longer so easy to reach the lodge and by the early seventeenth century it had fallen into disuse. It is still said, however, that there are tunnels underneath that site, and being off the beaten track it had, by the nineteenth century, become the legendary hideaway for the witches of the area.

Outside the forest is the village of Kelsall, where there once lived a witch named Ales Cauley. Ales is, in fact, a local spelling of the name Alice. It was said that the Devil often visited her in her lonely cottage. I am not sure if anyone ever saw this diabolical visitor, but it didn't put people off asking Ales for potions for their ailments. And some said that when they were at her cottage they had seen the toad.

It was said that a young man was travelling from Macclesfield to Chester. He was a young lover on his way to see his swaddledidaff, and to ask her father for her hand in marriage. However, he was not used to travelling alone and had left his home a little late. As the evening started to draw in, he soon became aware that he had wandered off the main road and was now lost. He had no idea which direction to go and decided to ask for help at a small cottage, which he could see through the trees. He knocked on the door and could only hear a croaking voice from somewhere inside the house shouting, 'Go away!'

Knowing that there was someone inside, he was determined to get some directions and so he knocked on the door again, this time louder and harder. Again a croaky old voice answered him, 'Go away!'

The young man was desperate to be on his way, but he needed to know which way and so this time he bent down and shouted through the keyhole, 'I do not wish to disturb you much more, but I am lost. I need to get back to the road. How do I get to Chester from here?'

Again the croaky old voice answered him, but this time she said, 'I am in bed already. I am not coming down. Now … go away!'

The young man would not go. He was sure he could get the old woman to tell him the directions, even if she was to shout them from the upstairs window. And so he continued banging on the door and shouting through the keyhole.

Finally, Ales Cauley got out of bed, but she wasn't happy with this impudent young man. She was determined not to give him directions now, even if she was slowly making her way down the stairs.

With his eye to the keyhole, the young man saw some movement and, thinking it was the old woman coming to open the door, he called out more and more. However, once at the bottom of the staircase she just stood at the door shouting, 'Go away! Leave me alone!'

The young man continued shouting and pleading, telling the old woman of how much he loved this girl and all his plans to marry her. But Ales was not impressed. She simply wanted to go to bed in peace. Until in the end, she had had enough. She threw out her arm, pointed at the door and then shouted, 'Why don't you hop off, young man!'

In an instant, the shouting stopped. There was no more pleading. No more banging. Ales breathed a sigh and hobbled up to the door itself. She unlocked it, opened it and, of course, there was no young man standing there any more. He had 'hopped off'.

Well, that's not quite true. He had certainly 'hopped', but not 'off'. Ales looked down and saw on the doorstep there was a small chubby toad.

'Ahh,' she sighed, 'So you became a toad. Well, we can't leave you out here.' And reaching down she picked up the bleary-eyed creature and brought it into the house. There on the table was an old mug. She plopped the toad into the mug and then carried it upstairs with her. And from that day on, she kept the toad in the mug under her bed. She would feed it flies, which she caught on her window sill, but she never let it go.

Finally, Ales Cauley died and the toad was able to crawl out of the mug and make its way out of the cottage. That toad had once been a young man travelling to Chester to ask his true love's father if he could marry the girl of his dreams. And so, the toad hopped off to find his swaddledidaff and her father. But Kelsall to Chester is a long way for a toad and it had been many years since he had first knocked at the door of Ales Cauley. Maybe, that toad is still hopping along, still trying to find his way.

Other women said to be witches were not as easily tolerated as the Witch of Kelsall. Many were hanged in the seventeenth century, when there seemed to be a paranoia over witchcraft, with demons suspected around every corner. Those hanged for being witches include Anne Thornton of Eaton, Ellen Beech of Macclesfield and Mary Baguley of Wildboarclough, who

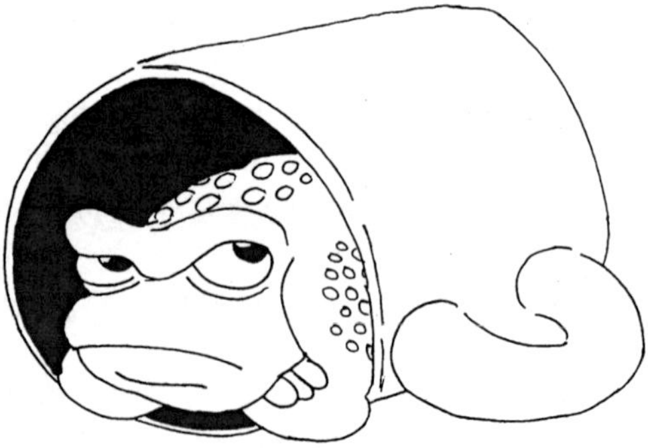

was charged with killing a man named Robert Hall through witchcraft at Wincle.

By the nineteenth century it seems that old women purported to be witches, such as Ales Cauley, were seen more as part of village life, performing a valuable function in alternative medicine. The most famous in Cheshire was probably Bridget Bostock of Coppenhall, who was reported on in the papers of the time. She is said to have catered for 160 patients per week, who came to her from as far as Nantwich in the south-west and Macclesfield in the north-east. She was known for using prayer and spittle in her healing rituals and refused payment, making her money as a housekeeper for one of the local families. I don't know how she managed to fit in all those patients or how she managed to produce enough saliva.

I have also heard that Murdishaw in Runcorn refers to the hanging place for criminals. The suffix 'shaw' being an old Cheshire word for 'wood' and the name therefore originally being 'Murder Shaw' or 'the killing wood'. If a gallows did stand here, then it may not be a big stretch of the imagination to suppose that those accused of witchcraft would have been hanged there also. Tales float around of a witch who was hanged somewhere in the area. It is said that, if you drive down Keckwick Lane then her spirit suddenly appears racing alongside the vehicle, trying to get in as she pulls on the door handles. I guess that this is where central locking comes in handy!

Twenty-one

The Image House

The greatest tale of the dark arts in Cheshire arguably involves a man, but not a wizard. Merlin himself may wait under Alderley Edge with the forces of King Arthur. And, the most powerful Cheshire wizard may be John o'th'Hill, who was feared by the witches of the county. However, I am referring to one who began life as a poacher and later turned to magic, leaving a lasting mark on the county. His story is retold in the novel written by Beatrice Tunstall during the 1930s. Entitled *The Shiny Night*, this book not only gives a fascinating overview of the folklore and traditions of Cheshire in Victorian times, but also tells the tale of the creator of the Image House. This mysterious house on the A49 outside of Bunbury has come to be very much associated with this novel, for those who know about it. But as to whether Tunstall drew on folklore for this tale, or created the whole thing from her imagination, no one is sure. It is said that Beatrice did change the names of the locations and characters for her book so as to protect their identities, which only serves to make the whole question more intriguing.

It is the story of the master poacher, Seth Shone, who was shipped off to Australia for manslaughter. Whilst on that long journey, chains on his wrists, Shone made a vow to God that he would return to England and wreak revenge on his enemies, these being the squire, the gamekeeper and several of his men. Seven years later, Shone appeared back in the area but he had changed. His hair was now completely white. This did shock folk initially, but there would be stranger happenings to come that would make them forget the shade of his hair.

Seth determined first of all to gain somewhere to live. There was a curious loophole in the laws of the land at that time, dating back to the favours granted to archers. It was that, if a man could build a dwelling on a piece of land without being stopped, and if he should have smoke going up through a chimney, then he could live on that land and could not be moved on. This was known as the building of Jeremies.

With the help of his friends, Shone built the makeshift house in one night, and by the time he was discovered, he had a fire going with smoke billowing out of the chimney. He then stood there, gun in hand, saying that if anyone tried to move him on, he would shoot and they would be lying six feet under in the local graveyard.

Now he had his land, Seth worked on making his house more comfortable, but he never forgot his dubious vow to God and determined how he might get revenge on his enemies. For this he turned to the dark arts, namely that of waxing. It is said that, if you know how to mix the wax, say the magic words and include a part of someone's hair or clothing in the mix, and then you mould the wax into a shape that represents that person, you will have put them under a curse. This is what Shone wanted to do, but to add to the menace, he wanted everyone to know who he had cursed. Therefore he prepared to cast the shapes with clay instead of wax. Following the occult rituals, he made images of his enemies, which he then fixed to the outside walls of his house for all to see. A visual threat to those he had chosen to be his victims.

The house was soon known as the Image House and all those depicted on its walls received an untimely death. But Seth did not escape in his dealings with the occult. As always, there is a pay back when you mess with such powers. Although Seth's spells seemed to work, it was not all as he had hoped.

Some of the images are still there on the walls of the Image House, while others are held at the Grosvenor Museum in Chester. They are fairly crude representations of the intended victims, looking more like gingerbread men in pointed hats than gamekeepers or landed gentry. But there is a curious porch on the house, which is said to be carved with the face of the Devil on each of its two wooden supports. I said before how no one seems to be sure whether Beatrice Tunstall created the tale of Seth Shone herself, or whether she drew on local folklore or historical records. However, the house is very clearly there and certainly fits the ideas presented in *The Shiny Night* – sometimes that's enough.

Twenty-two

Mermaids and Mere-maids

There was once a sailor whose name was John Robinson. He was not an old man but he had travelled to countries all across the world and he had seen many things. In all that time he had never taken a wife and so, whenever he returned to England, he would stay with his mother at the little village of Liscard on the Wirral Peninsula. Now, she was a widow, once the wife of a seafarer herself, yet she had grown up further inland in Cheshire, being from Little Bollington. She often worried about her son being out at sea, because it was on such a voyage that her husband had been lost. So, when her son returned and came to stay with her, she was always full of relief and joy to see her strong and adventurous boy. But the years were passing and still he had no wife and, of course, there were no grandchildren.

Now a wife was not greatly on John's mind, but there was one thing he particularly wanted – a female of another type. You see, being a mariner, John had heard countless tales of mermaids. He had heard of them singing on the rocks, enticing menfolk to bring their ships in too close. They would, of course, then crash and so arrive at a watery death. He had heard of the beauty of these mermaids and how they were half-woman and half-fish. He had also heard of others whose fishy tails turned into legs at night, so that they might walk in the land of humans. Even though he had heard all these stories, he had never seen a mermaid for himself and this is what he wanted more than many other things the world had to offer.

John was about to leave again for the high seas, his name being on the list of crew for a ship sailing out from Birkenhead. He only had one or two days more with his mother, and, as often happens with these things, he heard tell of a mermaid that had been sighted nearby. It was as he was walking along the coast between Wallasey and Leasowe that he happened upon an old fisherman who soon came to mention how a friend of his had spied a mermaid up on the rocks the previous night, along the shore that ran beside the Mockbeggars Hall.

'Aye,' he said, 'it was as he was coming in from a night of fishing. He tells me that she was up on the rocks there, combing her hair and singing to herself. Saw her as plainly as you sees me now, so he said.'

John could not contain himself. He asked for more details, the exact location, the time of night, the nature of the mermaid. Of course, the fisherman could only go on what his friend had said. In the end he laughed, saying to John, 'It's probably just one of those seals that comes up here every so often – lying back in the sun on the rocks and singing so sweetly. Ha-ha, he's always been tone deaf, that old friend of mine. He'd say a seagull sings like a nightingale, he would.'

But the idea of a mermaid there on the shore fired John's imagination and his passions. Knowing he had only a day left on the Wirral, he raced home with all sorts of ideas running through his head.

His mother was quite taken aback to see him bursting into the house. She was then completely flabbergasted when she heard what had excited him so, and his plans to take a boat out that night and row along the coast to find the mermaid for himself.

Sitting down in almost a faint she said, 'Please John, please, don't go out there looking for that monster. You don't know what you're playing with, messing about with inhuman folk like that.'

'But mother, what harm can come? This is something I have wanted to see all my life and I am only going to look. The old fisherman said she was simply combing her hair and singing to herself. She wasn't trying to lure sailors to their death.'

His mother sighed, her face looking long and drawn as she heard the determination in her son's voice.

'John, listen to me. There are mermaid folk popping up in all sorts of places around Cheshire, surprising places, but the story is always the same. It just brings trouble and grief for those that go out looking for them.' And she then went on to tell her son a story she had often heard.

'You see John, down in the village of Wrenbury they've got a church and the bells of that church were actually from the old abbey at Combermere. When Henry VIII took over and the monasteries were all dissolved, the bells of Combermere Abbey were taken down and thrown into the mere itself. Being such heavy things they sank down into the depths and that was that, or so everyone thought.'

'But then many years later, someone had the bright idea of retrieving those bells and putting them up in the church at Wrenbury. Now, the parson had warned the men who had the job that they had to be careful. See, he knew that down in the depths of that water there lived a spirit of some sorts, a mere-maid he called it. And he said that those labourers would be all right so long as they kept their language clean. No cursing and no lewd talk and such like. Well, somehow, I don't know how they did it, but somehow, they managed to get some ropes tied on to those bells and pull them up one by one and into the boats. But they're right heavy things and one of them was almost up in the boat when it slipped from their grasp and splashed into the water again. That workman who was in the boat was not happy. It had been such a palaver getting that bell up from the water and now they had to start again. And before he could think twice about what he was saying, a curse leaked out from his lips. And you know he shouldn't have done that, because no sooner had the words skimmed out over the water, than a long, thin arm shot up out of the mere and over the side of the boat. That workman was grabbed and pulled overboard. He disappeared below the surface never to be seen again. And that was a mere-maid, that was.'

John shook his head to hear his mother telling him such tales, as if he was five not thirty-five. 'Mother, listen to ya,' he sighed, 'supposing that's all true, then that mere-maid or mermaid or what-you-like was reacting to the curse from that labourer. There's no reason to think the same thing is going to happen with the mermaid off the coast here. 'Sides, this is the sea not the meres of Cheshire.'

'And that labourer paid no attention to warnings!' snapped the mariner's mother, 'and the warnings of a parson too. You ought to listen to your elders young Johnny. You're not too old for me to tell you when you're heading off on a road to ruin.'

'Mother, mother,' John sighed, 'there's no need to fret so. Don't you know about the mermaid of Rostherne Mere? Your tale of Combermere has just gone and reminded me of that and I've been in half-a-mind to make the journey down Knutsford way and see this creature for myself, and would have done if I had been here over Eastertide.'

'Then thank Heaven that you've been here only this summertime,' cried the mother, 'and don't you be telling me about tales of Cheshire when I've been here many more days than you, with all your gallivanting overseas like your father.'

'But mother,' John tried to calm her now, 'am I right in thinking that the mermaid of Rostherne Mere is a kinder creature, even a God-fearing one?'

His mother stopped and considered. 'So they say,' she had to admit, 'but listen, it's all to do with lost bells. One of the bells from the church there, St Mary's I think it was, it was so heavy and the fixings hadn't been looked after, so that when they were pealing away one Easter Sunday, the heaviest bell broke off its fixing, came crashing down through the tower, rolled out through the door and down the hill to the water's edge. How no one was killed must be by the grace of God. Well, that week a gang of men tried to bring that bell back up to the church, but every time they got it up the hill, it'd slip from them and roll all the way back down again. Until, the third time it happened, one of their number cursed the bell, when I'm sure he would have been warned afore not to, and it rolled this time down into the mere itself, sinking right down to the bottom. Now at Eastertide, the bell can be heard ringing from way down in those depths and who rings it to affright the local people so? One of your mermaids. This 'un comes from the seas, so they say. Through an underground waterway that leads from the River Mersey all the way to Rostherne Mere. A proper mermaid, scaring folk by ringing that bell once a year.'

'And I heard, Mother, that on Easter Sunday there's a new voice in the church choir. A beautiful young woman, who sings sweeter than any in the village, or even in the county. She joins the blessed congregation to celebrate the Lord's Resurrection, having risen from the waters herself, and then returns to the mere once she's celebrated the highest of all holy days.'

'Maybe she does, maybe she doesn't,' mumbled the widow, 'but what a sight that'd be. A moistened wench, flipping and flopping through the church with her fishy tail, disgracing the House of God.'

'I heard that she grows legs when she climbs up out of the water.'

'That as may be, but she'd still be dripping away on the rushes there. And Heaven forbid to think what she'd be wearing … or not wearing, more like.'

John laughed at his mother's dismissal of the mermaid, but she was not happy.

'Listen here, my boy,' she continued, 'you may well laugh at me, but if you want to see a mermaid, you may as well get on that ship you're on the list for and have a look out there as you sail about the Seven Seas. There's no use you wasting your time splashing about here looking, after some tale from the friend of a friend of a drunken fisherman. And that's all I'm saying.'

Then, she was up and out, saying she had washing to hang up whilst there was a good wind to get it dry. And John was left to contemplate the mermaids of Cheshire, and what he should do during those final hours before sailing away.

It was the very next night that John Robinson left Liscard and made his way to Leasowe. He had spent that afternoon away from his mother's house, as he knew she would again try to convince him to stay and not go looking for mermaids. He needed to find a boat anyway, which he figured would keep him busy. In his contemplations, he had decided that this would be the last chance to find the fabled creature before he was shipped out again. And so, he hired a small rowing boat in the end and headed out from Leasowe along the coast, with a lantern tied on to the little prow. There was a wind blowing and soon the clouds were swept back to reveal the moon looking down over the sea. The perfect night for looking out for mermaids, he hoped. As his oars sploshed back and forth, dipping into the briny, up and out again, John focused on the rocky area where he had been told the mermaid had been sighted. There was no movement there. Just the waves gently, almost half-heartedly, stroking the stones. He sat and watched for hours, and still nothing appeared, until the chill off the water had become too much for him, even though he was wrapped in a blanket. And so he decided that the fisherman's tale must have been an exaggeration. Maybe it had been one of those seals that come up every so often after all. So, John took the oars to set off back along the coast to the Mersey estuary.

It was just as he was about to enter the estuary, his boat lightly bobbing on the surface of the water, that a soft high song floated out and touched the ears of that sailor. John looked about frantically. Scanning the shore in the moonlight, he tried to spot where the singer may be, whoever it was. And there, lit by the midnight moon, sat on Black Rock on the northernmost tip of the Wirral Peninsula was a glistening silhouette – a female form running her fingers through her long hair as she looked up to the sky and sang what sounded to be a sad song in a tongue unknown to John, or any other person in England if truth be told.

Easing the oars gently through the water, but trembling with excitement, John turned the boat towards Black Rock and began to move over the waves, with the woman's voice rising in his ears – a sweet sound, drawing him closer. And then she stopped and their eyes met. John froze. Would his presence now scare her away? He dared do nothing more. He did not want to frighten her, nor suggest he was up to no good. But now he could see her – a slender figure with long wet but curiously straight hair, and instead of legs she had the tail and the scales of a fish. The mermaid tilted her head slightly as she stared at the sailor, weighing him up, wondering what he might be or what his intentions were. And it was now that John spoke. Making his voice as light as possible, he allowed his words to echo over the water.

'Don't be afraid,' he cooed, 'I only want to look at you. Never seen a mermaid afore. I'm not gonna hurt you.'

The mermaid tilted her head to the other side and looked puzzled. However, her eyes were still fixed to John's and this gave him the impression that she was going to stay. He was therefore disappointed the next second when she suddenly looked away, slid off the rock and smoothly disappeared into the sea, leaving no trace on the water's surface except for a few momentary bubbles. John sighed and looked at the now empty rocks. He was about to pull the boat closer when suddenly it lurched to one side. He turned and saw a hand was holding on to the edge of the boat. Then another joined it. Then there appeared a head of hair, dripping wet. Two dark eyes rose up, followed by a small, gentle face. It was the mermaid and the boat lurched again as she pulled herself up and over, her fishy tail flopping on to the boards. And there they were – John's dream come true. He was face to face with a mermaid who had now settled in his boat. He was unable to say anything at first, and his dumb state continued as he saw the mermaid's fishy tail transform before his eyes. The scales smoothed themselves out and the tail looked as if it was being remoulded by unseen hands, reformed into a pair of slender legs with the daintiest feet John had ever seen. And now, sat in the boat, was the prettiest woman he had ever known. John had known many women in his time, some of them a lot fishier than this mermaid, but despite his past, he knew that he ought to treat a woman with respect and so he picked up a blanket that was in the boat and offered it to the girl. She looked at him in curiosity, but he wasn't put off. John shook out the blanket and leant over to gently drape it around the mermaid's shoulders and so guard her modesty.

Then he sat back and almost fell into the water when the mermaid whispered, 'Thank-you.'

'Y-y-you can speak English?' he asked amazed.

'I speak many languages of humankind,' she answered, looking deep into his eyes. 'What manner of man are you?' she asked.

'My name is John,' he said, 'I'm a seafarer, maybe like yourself, though I fare on top of the sea.'

The mermaid smiled and it was the brightest, friendliest smile John had ever seen.

'Do you have a name?' he asked.

She nodded then whispered a long sound to the sailor which sounded like the wind moving over the waves, 'Nesssssssssssssssssssss.'

'Ness?' asked John.

She raised her thin eyebrows and nodded. Then suddenly she looked away, as if John's gaze made her self-conscious, as if she was shy.

John tried to keep the conversation going.

'I've always heard of mermaids, but never seen one until today,' he said. 'You live along this coast?'

She nodded while still looking at the floor of the gently rocking vessel. 'But, I do explore the tunnels under the land there.' And she tilted her head towards the coast.

Tunnels? John remembered what his mother had said when they talked about Rostherne Mere. 'Are you the mermaid that appears at Rostherne?'

Ness looked puzzled.

'The mere with the bell,' he ventured, 'you ring the bell under the water and then come up and join the choir?'

Ness' eyes brightened in recognition and laughed in sweet surprise, 'You know of this? Yes, each year I do this. I swim through the caverns leading from these waters to a place where there is a bell. I ring it, and then I make my way up on to the land to join with the humankind. I sing with them in their building.'

John laughed now, 'Then your fishy tail changes there also, so that you can walk into the church?'

'Of course, how else could I move about on land?'

From this point on, the two in the boat laughed and talked about the land thereabouts and the legends John knew of, and the other creatures Ness knew of. Ness was also aware of some of the stories about mermaids out at sea. She could suggest names for some of those watery women John mentioned, even though she herself stayed mainly around the Irish Sea. She preferred exploring the caves and tunnels along the British coast, rather than venturing out to the wide and warmer waters of the Seven Seas.

Time was passing as the two conversed until Ness stopped and said, 'I must make sure I do not stay too long. The sun must not catch me here above the water. If it does then I will be no more.'

'What do you mean?' asked John. 'The sun will do damage to you?'

'It will. I will melt and be no more.'

'But what about when you sing in the choir at the church on Eastertide?'

The mermaid looked puzzled, 'I come up out of the water when it is dark,' she answered, 'there is no sun when I come up to sing.'

Now John looked puzzled.

'I join the choir which gathers in the night, then when the first bird sings to announce the Easter morn I return to the water of the mere, before the sun can rise and end my life.'

John leant back against the boat and chuckled. 'How the tales of folk get all mixed up. The story I heard was that you were in the choir for Easter morning. How things change from mouth to mouth.'

Ness smiled too, but seemed to have something else on her mind and looked about their surroundings. The boat had drifted somewhat from Black Rock, but John had not noticed, he was too taken up with Ness.

'Listen to my tale, John,' she then said, 'how we merfolk know to be wary of the sun. There was one of our number – an asrai – who met one of your kind when he was out fishing. The asrai was suddenly pulled up from the lakebed as a net had come over her. It had been dragged along the bottom of the water and our cousin was caught in it. She tried to struggle free, but the more she struggled the more she became entangled. Until, finally, the net was pulled up out of the water and the asrai fell on to the deck of the boat like a fish. The man in the boat, a fisher from humankind, eyed her and seemed amazed to see her. But then, she was not as human-looking as me. The asrai are smaller, looking like children, with green hair and webbed hands and feet. She begged to be set free and returned to the water, but the fisherman could not bring himself to lose what he considered to be a rare and magical creature. The asrai cried and warned him that the sun would come up soon and that would mean death to her, but he just wanted to look at her a little longer. She wiggled and writhed and managed to get one hand out from the net. In desperation, she reached over to him and clutched his arm, begging again to be returned. But the touch of an asrai is chilling to a human and the fisherman leapt back from her, cradling his now freezing arm. He rubbed that arm over and over to get it warm again, and all this time the morning sun was coming closer. He decided some exercise would help, and so he started to row the boat to the shore. The asrai could hear him saying how much his children would like to see this creature, and how there would be some who would pay much money for a viewing also. All this time the asrai pleaded and pleaded until the sun did rise.'

At this point, Ness stopped her story and looked around again. It was still night there, off the Wirral Peninsula, and so she continued her tale.

'When the fisherman reached the shore, the sun had arisen. He noticed now how quiet it was in his boat. No more pleading or begging from the asrai. He turned around and all he saw was the net with a few of the mere's weeds caught up in it. He pushed the bundle to one side and found that there was a puddle on the deck of the boat. Some of it was thick with a green jelly and some just water. The asrai had been touched by the sun's rays and she was …'

The mermaid's voice trailed off and she looked down again, at her feet.

'She was melted?' continued John.

Ness nodded.

'And you believe that's what'll happen to you?'

Ness nodded again.

'Then you must return and soon I think,' he said, looking out across the waves at a thin line of gold, which was lining the horizon.

Ness looked up and gasped. 'You are right,' she said, 'I must go.'

Even though John had seen the first light of the morning, he didn't really want to lose his mermaid. Yet what good would it be if she stayed and then turned to mush? He looked appealingly to Ness and she stared at him, holding his eyes with hers until she said, 'Let me fetch you something by which you will remember me.'

'I don't think I'm gonna forget you,' he said with a sigh.

She smiled, but hastily Ness reached to her hand where she was wearing a ring. Quickly, she twisted it until it came off and then she handed the ring to John.

'Here, take this and remember me,' she said. John turned the object in his hand. It was formed from a green twisted metal and set with a single black stone. He could see that something had been cut into the stone, a design of some sort. It looked to be a collection of circles intertwined, but not just a pattern. The circles formed one shape together, but he just could not make it out. As he turned the ring in his hand, Ness told him more.

'This is a ring from the forest which now lies under the waters. People of your kind used to dwell there until the sea reclaimed her land. In those days, human people would come into the woods and make offerings to us. One of those was this ring. Keep it and remember me. You have dreamt of meeting a mermaid and this night the dream has become truth. As the sun now rises, I must go, but you John can now join those others who say that they have seen my kind. I shall never forget this night and your kindness. Keep the ring, for very few can say they possess an object given to them by a mermaid.'

And before any words of thanks or gratitude could escape John's lips, the mermaid had slipped over the side of the boat and into the water to disappear beneath the waves.

John looked over into the depths but could see no trace of Ness anywhere. The sun had risen quickly, yet the sky was changing from blue to grey. He held the ring up to the light from the rising sun and suddenly he could see what it was. Those circles, scratched into the stone, all worked together to show the shape of a skull. He hadn't expected that. Curious, he thought, as he noticed that a wind was rising and the boat was beginning to be rocked more forcibly by the waves. He looked up and could no longer see Black Rock. In fact, he could hardly see the shore. In the time when he and the mermaid had been conversing, the boat had drifted far and he had not noticed. It felt as if there was a storm coming. The sun may have come up, but the clouds had quickly covered it and the sky was black again. The waves rose higher and rain started to pelt down, water on water. John quickly shoved the ring on to his little finger so that he wouldn't lose it. Then he grabbed the oars and, through the wind and the rain, and fighting the waves, he pulled and pulled to make it back to shore.

It was a fatigued and soaked John that arrived back at his mother's cottage in Liscard. He was shivering with cold, and so quickly got out of his wet clothing to sit by the stove, whilst his mother rushed about to fix him with some hot tea – all the time cursing her son's decision and tutting over how he was supposed to go to sea that day. Whilst John, wrapped up and trying to get warm, looked at the ring there on his little finger. He had thought that the mermaid, Ness, had not meant him any harm. Yet here was a ring marked with a skull, which she had given him. He was a little perturbed about that, but maybe it was a sign of the people who had once visited those woods now under the waves. It may not be anything harmful. He suddenly coughed and blew his nose again. His mother rushed over and placed her hand on his forehead.

'And you've got a fever. I told you not to go out there. Those mermaids are nought but trouble,' she continued as she went to wet a cloth to place on his forehead.

John did not go out to sea that day, as you can probably guess. He sailed away in a delirium on his bed, as his condition worsened. His poor mother did what she could and the doctor visited regularly, but nothing improved. It was whilst she was sitting at her son's side that she noticed the ring on his little finger. She had not seen it before and rightly suspected it had come from the mermaid. She tried to remove it, but it was stuck firm. She panicked now and when the doctor came she asked him to give it a go. The doctor was not so concerned, believing more in medicine and science, rather than magical rings and mermaids, but he was a kind man and made an attempt. He was unable to remove it.

It was within twenty-four hours from that instant that John Robinson died. His poor mother was now left without anyone in Liscard. No husband, no son and certainly no grandchildren and so she went back to Little Bollington, as far away from the sea as she could be. However, just before, when the undertakers came to prepare John's body, they noticed that lying on the floor under the bed there was a curious green ring with a black stone. They asked Mrs Robinson about it and her face tightened.

'So it comes off now that my son is dead. Throw it away! Get rid of it! It's no good and I want nowt to do with it.'

It was one of the undertakers who happened to place that ring in his pocket – and he almost forgot about it, until one day when he was walking along the coast, somewhere near Leasowe. He saw off Dove Point some curious shapes in the water, like trees made of stone, and all of a sudden a strange sensation came over him. It was as if his pocket was moving, leaning forward to those

petrified tree stumps below the waves. Reaching into his pocket, he pulled out that ring from the Robinson house and threw it into the water. And now, he wasn't sure if he really saw this or not, but there was suddenly the fleeting glance of a woman passing through the water. She caught the ring before it hit the sandy bed and then was gone. He says he did not see it clearly, and it may have been the reflection of a cloud passing overhead, but if he did see a woman, she had a tail like a fish, like a mermaid.

Maybe if you were to wander along Mockbeggars Wharf even today, you would hear the sweet singing of Ness, or perhaps you would bump into her should you be at Rostherne Church the night before Easter Sunday. Or maybe you will just hear the bell ringing up from the depth of the mere, for mermaid or mere-maid, she seems to have avoided the light from the sun, and is remembered in this corner of England to this day.

Twenty-three

GINNY GREEN TEETH

It seems that adults have always warned children away from dangerous places, such as mines, ponds and dark places, by using stories or with warnings of bogeyman-like creatures. All over Cheshire there seem to be traces of a treacherously mischievous creature known as a hob or hob-dross. Throughout the county there are places named Hobhill in honour of the goblin-like sprites, which are said to cause havoc in the region. But a hob-dross is more of a water-bound goblin. With so many wet and boggy places, children would be warned to take care, and the hob-dross would, of course, be a helpful deterrent. There are also the boggarts. A boggart is often known as a spirit that can change its shape, but for Cheshire, the boggart is generally a female creature which inhabits watery regions. Waiting beneath the duckweed, the boggart is always ready for those who wander too close, thinking the green before them is grass. Then a slimy hand will shoot up through the water and pull the unsuspecting person in, and they are never seen again.

The most notorious of them all is Ginny Green Teeth. Sometimes known as Jennie or Jinny, her notoriety has spread north of the Mersey, and south to parts of Shropshire. There are many tales of this malevolent spirit, whose favourite shape is that of a skinny old woman with long white hair. She has also been represented as a charming green fairy, as well as a crocodile-like creature lurking in the shallows. One tale told in Warrington is of how she would steal the souls of old men, handing their bodies over to her sister boggarts in the waters. But I am often requested to tell the story of the children who thought to defy their parents' warnings one Halloween.

Children in the area had grown up with the warnings of Ginny Green Teeth and so had learnt to keep away from the water, but no child had actually seen her. There was one young man, named Harry, for whom this was too great a temptation. If such a creature existed, he wanted to see her, and he would often say so to his friends. He would boast about how he was determined to find her for himself and that they ought to come with him. They, of course, were more sensible than that, heeding the warnings, and so put him off from purposely going out to find the boggart, which could only lead to trouble. That was until one Halloween night. The children were all out for 'Trick or Treat', and this gang was no exception. They had their costumes on and one of them, Edward, carried a lantern carved from a pumpkin. However, seeing as they were allowed out and there were no parents overseeing them, young Harry decided that this night would be the perfect opportunity to go down to the pit and see if old Ginny Green Teeth was about. His friends tried to protest, but he was such a determined young man, and called them 'Chicken' so much, that they felt ashamed. It was against their better judgement then, that they all headed off, the five of them, leaving the houses behind and passing through the gate into the nearby woods where there was a sniddlebog.

'Come on,' said Harry, 'there's no need to worry. You know, if you can see her then you know where she is. If she's in front of us, then she can't be behind us, can she? We'll approach the pit carefully and all keep an eye out.'

This they did, slowly and carefully. Some slower and with more care than others.

The moon shone down from a cloudless sky and its reflection seemed to light up the little pond. The duckweed which spread over the surface looked like a grey blanket against the black water, and the sniddle leaves were edged with a cold silvery light.

'See, there's nothing here,' said one boy finally, keen to get back home.

'We're missing out on the sweets anyway,' said another.

'Wait,' said Harry, 'there's something moving in the weed.' And he pointed across the water to a shimmering shape, which seemed to be moving up through the grey mass. It looked like a new clump of duckweed suddenly rising up from the depths. But soon the boys realised what it was. It was a head of hair coming up from under the water, face down.

'It's Ginny Greeth Teeth!' screeched one child, but the others could say nothing as more of the figure started to rise up from the water, showing that the head did, in fact, have a body. There was the person's back bobbing up through the water and it was clear that they were wearing a dress.

'Our Jane has a dress like that,' gasped one child, 'It's not Ginny Green Teeth. That's our Jane!'

All the children stared at the body in the water. Was he right? Slowly, ever so slowly, the girl in the water seemed to be moving. Slowly her head started to rise, despite the weed caught there. And slowly two hands slid out of the water.

'It is our Jane. It is!' persisted the child.

Those hands reached up as 'our Jane' sat in the water facing the boys in the moonlight, from the far edge of the pond. Those hands swept her hair back off her face, and then all the boys gasped again. For there was no face, no mouth, no nose, no eyes. Under that hair there was simply the blank front of a head.

'Her soul has been taken,' Harry whispered under his breath.

'Our Jane,' softly moaned the other child.

'Childerrrrrrr,' hissed a husky voice from behind the gang.

The children froze. Who was that messing about?

'Chiiiiiilder,' it hissed again and now sounded pleased.

The children turned to see who it was behind them.

'Chiiiiiiilderrrrrrrr …'

There was a flash of silver hair, the gleam of green teeth in the dark, and the scream of several children, followed by one almighty splash.

When the children did not return after 'Trick or Treat', their parents became worried. And so they set off to find out where their sons had got to.

'Up to no good!' said one.

'Anything could've happened,' said another.

But even though they knocked at every door, no one could say that they had seen them. The parents went beyond the houses and through the gate to the woods. Down the path, they went calling the names of their lost little ones, until they all arrived at the pit. The moon shone down from a cloudless sky and its reflection seemed to light up the little pond. The duckweed which spread over the surface looked like a grey blanket over the black water and the sniddle leaves were edged with a cold silvery light. And there was nothing else to note except for a lantern carved from a pumpkin, which was floating alone on the surface of the water.

Twenty-four

The Sands of Dee

It's amazing that a landlocked county, such as Cheshire, has so many tales and songs about people being lost to drowning, but of course, the Wirral is surrounded by water on three sides. There are numerous tales of people being surprised by changes in the tide and losing their life as a result. The River Mersey, especially, has a large tidal range, which can rise to be over 10m. Its flow can be confusing and therefore dangerous to small craft. Similarly, the sea rises up quickly at the western corner of the Wirral, where the River Dee emerges. And so the folk songs continue to tell of the tragic adventures of those who found death on the sea, or in the rivers of this already wet county.

The island of Hilbre (pronounced 'hill-bree') has lured the curious and intrepid into danger many times, both in the past and in modern times. Standing just off Hoylake, Hilbre is accompanied by a handful of smaller islands known as the Red Rocks. These little islands all look close and easy to get to. Added to that, the flat sand suggests that one can make a fair guess at when the tide is coming in. However, many have been caught out as they have walked across the sands. The sea can creep up behind you and cut off all hope of returning safely.

It wasn't until the 1970s that a supposedly 'safe' route from Red Rocks was closed. Visitors are now advised to follow a safer route from West Kirby. The route to and from the island of Hilbre has been known for its risks for hundreds of years. Both song and memory speak of a young woman often referred to as Mary. She lived on Hilbre, where her family reared cattle. Mary had beautiful red hair, which she rarely tied back when riding. Her flame-like locks would fly in the coastal winds, billowing out to the side like a hundred red ribbons. The sight was even more enthralling when she rode her strawberry roan horse. This beast had red hair too, and its long mane would blow in the wind so that it came together with Mary's hair; you couldn't tell where one ended and the other began. It was almost as if some magical spirit was making its way across the sand, a captivating combination of both horse and rider.

Now, Mary was often seen bringing the cattle across the sands of the Dee for the market at West Kirby. Many had commented on her fairy-like appearance with the horse. She should have known the signs of the tide very well; she had been across that stretch of sand many times. One particular morning, the young woman mounted her horse to lead the cattle once again. The hooves slapped over the wet sand and the wind blew across the broad open landscape. Mary brushed the hair out of her face and looked at the coastline stretching out in front of her. She looked to the left and right, throwing her head back as she did to see what the tide was up to. Mary could see in the distance the flicker of sunlight on water, indicating that the western tide was creeping along the coast, round and round, gradually moving in closer and closer. Mary guessed that if she kept on towards West Kirby, she would make it with no problems. After all, she had made this crossing many times before. So she called out to the cattle, keeping them moving, keeping them with her. Her mother had watched her set out, and could hear her daughter's voice calling over the sands of the Dee.

People ashore went about their daily business along the beach. The families of fishermen helped with the nets and the selling of fish. Others were washing down their boats, removing the tangled seaweed. All of them had seen the red hair of both girl and horse intermingling in the wind many times. She had always safely made the crossing in the past, but few saw how today the tide was moving quicker, round and round, closer and closer to the girl. Mary geed up the horse and called again for the cows to quicken their pace. But suddenly a mist floated over the sea, as if it was in cahoots with the waves. Like a great white blanket, the mist rolled over Mary, her horse, and the cattle; all were hidden from sight. Mary's mother was about to return to the house, fishermen were about to put away their nets, others were about to duck down to wash their boats, when they all became aware that the bright red hair of horse and girl were no longer in view. The whole community stopped for that moment, wondering where young Mary could be. There was no voice calling the cattle. All held their breath, adding to the eerie silence. Suddenly, the wind rose and the mist was blown away. They could again see shapes heading towards the shore. The herd of cattle splashed across the beach, led now by a riderless horse. As the beasts hastened to outrun the rising waves, the cry of a mother echoed across the water. Boats were manned and pushed out into the water in a panic. Folk gathered on the shore, hoping that the search was not too late. Rowing furiously, the fishermen took with them their nets. They were heading out with hope against hope to bring in a different fish this morning. Looking about for any sign of the girl, the men fought against the tide until someone called out. There, at the fishing stakes, was something floating, caught on the stationary nets. Pulling the boats in closer, the sun highlighted the red of the swaying object. It was not a salmon. It was not seaweed. They all recognised the red locks of the girl they had seen so often, but it was only her hair. Where was Mary's body? The search continued throughout the day, but to no avail, and all the while a mother stood on Hilbre Island calling out for her daughter to come home.

As kindly folk took the mother into her abode, and the fishermen returned home with empty nets, the darkness of the night fell. The wind rose, whistling through the rocks and houses. The boats along the shore bobbed in the stirring waters and, as the chandlery jangled, a high-pitched voice could just about be heard in the distance. It was the sound of a girl calling her cattle, calling them to hurry up, urging them on. But there were no cattle coming across, and there was no longer any girl there on the sands of Dee. Only her voice remained.

During his years in Chester, Charles Kingsley may have heard of this legend and he wrote a poem about it which is one of the sources for my retelling of this tale. Kingsley's poem appears in his lesser-known novel, *Alton Locke*. However, the poem stands equally well alone, and has become a folk song in its own right, such is the power of Mary's tale of 'The Sands of Dee'.

Twenty-five

Thomas Clutterbuck and Polly Higginbotham

There was once a man of Chester who was not rich, but he liked the sound of his own voice. Not in the way of being a terrible bore, nor a great public speaker, but he was convinced he had an admirable singing voice. To be honest, his voice was not the worst in Chester, but it wasn't the best either. He could hold a tune, he could sing in key and he enjoyed singing, so who was to criticise him?

Now, it so happened that this man, Thomas Clutterbuck, had fallen in love. The beauty of a young Miss Polly Higginbotham had caught his eye and touched his heart. She was a rich young lady and so, Thomas knew that there would be much competition for her love. However, he also knew that there were not many who could sing as he did. So, what he lacked in finances, he hoped to make up for in vocal talents. He was flabbergasted when she accepted his proposal to take a boating trip together out on the River Dee, and so, one Sunday afternoon, that is what they did.

There was much playful chitchat on the little rowing boat that afternoon and throughout it all, Polly Higginbotham was wondering what this not unhandsome young man would do to win her over. He seemed nervous, and often looked about at the other vessels out on the river that day. But then her interest was piqued when Thomas told the waterman to row them over to a quieter point on the river. What was he up to? The waterman would still be in the boat with them, but such men were used to taking couples out on the river and finding something else to occupy their attention at certain moments on the trip.

Once they were away from the general Sunday boating crowd, Thomas stood up in the boat. Polly laughed as the boat rocked and she saw Thomas stagger, but she was intrigued as to what this was all leading to. Thomas then blew his nose, cleared his throat and began to sing:

There was a jolly miller lived on the River Dee
He worked and sang from morn till night, no lark so blithe as he
And this the burden of his song, forever used to be
'I care for nobody, no not I and nobody cares for me.'

Although Thomas did sing fairly well – I did say that his voice was not unpleasant – this was perhaps not the best choice he could have made. It was a song well known and sung by all. It was a song taught to children in school, and one which Polly had heard countless times before. Maybe Thomas had hoped he would bring his own touch to a familiar tune, or maybe he was warming up with something he knew well, before he launched into a more daring song which would truly declare the depths of his heart. Either way, it was lost on Polly. But she was not someone to be rude, coming from a good family, and she settled back in the boat as if she was enjoying the sound of Mr Clutterbuck's voice, allowing his dulcet tones to float over her.

That is very much the way Thomas saw it and so he continued through the classic – through all seven verses. And when he had finally finished, he saw that the object of his affections was still lying back with her eyes closed, caught up in the charming strains of his rendition. Encouraged therefore, Thomas moved on to a more daring song, one more of love. He decided to choose something he had heard from Shakespeare, to ensure

Polly knew of his reading and his finer tastes. And so he began to sing 'Oh, mistress mine', a song which he felt would call her to him, a song which would press on her to make the most of the opportunities presented to her.

As he sang, Thomas grew in courage and allowed himself to be caught up in the words of the great Bard. He closed his eyes and put his soul into those notes, like the nightingale singing to the moon:

Oh, wait and see thy true love's coming
Who can sing both high and low.

Thomas was so wrapped up in the song, and in the ambience he felt he had created, that he went through the whole rendition three times, until finally he came to the last line, for the final time:

Then, come kiss me, sweet and twenty,
Youth's a stuff will not endure.

And as his final note faded away, he felt something change in the boat. It rocked slightly, as if something had been thrown overboard. Thomas opened his eyes to address his love again and … she was gone. He couldn't believe it. Where Polly had been sitting, leaning back, enraptured by his mellifluous voice, there was now an empty board. Hastily he looked about. They were not near the bank, so she could not have got up and jumped on to dry land. He looked over the side. The water was too deep for wading back to shore. And why would she want to do either of those things? Thomas demanded of the waterman if he knew where the young woman had gone. But he had been suitably discreet; the waterman had been looking the other way, watching the cows on the distant bank. Thomas was, for a moment, decidedly flummoxed.

Whilst Thomas had been singing with his eyes closed, poor Polly had realised that she was about to be graced with no end of songs that she had heard countless times before. And there was no way of escaping. She had looked over the edge of the boat and her summary of the situation was confirmed. There was no way she could return to the bank without asking Thomas to take her back. Polly, although bored, was a kind soul, and did not want to upset the young man. So, she leant on the boat's side and looked out into the water to see if there were any fish or ducks she could watch. Anything rather than simply listen to Thomas' uncreative warbling.

The combination of tedium and the gentle rocking of the boat very soon put Polly to sleep. So now, had Thomas opened his eyes, he would have seen his love still there with her eyes closed, and supposed that she was caught up in his tuneful spell, reflecting on the beauty of his tone and pitch. But Thomas did not open his eyes, and did not notice his audience of one turn a little in her sleep, then turn too much and slip over the side of the boat. So caught up in his own singing was he, that Thomas did not even hear the splash as she hit the water and disappeared beneath the surface.

The truth of the situation suddenly dawned on Thomas, and he knew what had to be done. He paid the waterman, who'd had a number of surprises already that day, then leapt overboard, into the water, fully clothed. Thomas may have been an average singer, but he was a less than average swimmer. In his desperation to find his love, he allowed himself to sink lower and lower, towards the bottom of the river, looking about for his lost Polly. I don't know what happened next. Maybe his foot got caught in some weed, perhaps he banged his head on a rock, but the waterman on the surface did not see Thomas arise from the river. And so the courting couple were united, in the unseen world of the fishes, where it doesn't matter which song you choose to sing.

It is now said that, at night along the River Dee, as it runs through Chester, you may see two strange spirits stalking about – two river ghosts. One is said to have a head like a salmon and the other a tail like a mermaid. Unusual ghosts they are indeed, not confined to the river, but existing as a warning to all young lovers who should remember that 'the way to shun a watery death is by making love on dry land'.

Twenty-six

The Curst Fisherman

There was an old shrimper who had been watching a young fisherman wandering along the beach. The fisherman, William Lake, was known to him, but the old shrimper was a bit surprised to see him standing for a long time looking at something on the shore, caught up in a pile of seaweed. There had been a storm the night before and all sorts had been brought up on to the sand, including a good number of shrimp. However, the shrimper wondered what it was that William was looking at and decided to see for himself.

Just as he rose up from the pot he was sitting on, stretching his old salt-wrecked body, young William turned and ran back along the beach. He seemed in a good hurry for something and the old shrimper was unable to ask him about anything, too fast was he for the old man. So, the shrimper went to have a look at whatever it was caught up in the weed.

It took him some time to get there and, as he hobbled over, he got a good gradual look at the pile and was sure he could see a pair of boots. He was right, but the boots were still on the feet of someone. Caught up in the seaweed there was the corpse of a young man, another fisherman known to the old shrimper. It was John Stone, now as lifeless as his name suggested. The old shrimper tutted as he considered that John must have been out in the storm the previous night, and surmised that the waves had got the better of him. You never can tell what the sea will bring up on to the shore after a storm.

Now, there was a comely young girl who lived at Hoylake, whose name was Bessy Blake. She had received the attentions of two young men in recent months, but there was one she preferred over the other. She was hoping that he would come and see her that day. He was a fisherman, but with the storm that had been raging the night before, she suspected that he would not have been out fishing and so would not need to be at the market that morning. However, that young man was John Stone. He had been out, chancing his luck with the powers of nature, and he had lost. Naturally, when news of what had happened to John reached her, she was distraught and so were all those who knew the two of them.

All that is, bar William Blake. He was the other, young man who was vying for the love of Bessy Blake. As he had wandered along the beach that morning, the sky still grey after the storm, he wondered what he would find washed-up. He did not expect to find his rival caught in the seaweed. Now, it's said that if you discover a dead body from the waves, then it is your Christian duty to give the corpse a decent burial. Others say though that if the sea has taken a life, then the sea must keep the body. I'm not sure which of these views William held with, only that as he looked at the body of John Stone, something fell from that dead man's clasped hand. It was a sea-soaked book, one used for noting sales of fish. Nothing too surprising about that, only why would he be holding on to it out at sea? William picked up the book and, as he did, something fell from the back. It was a lock of hair, and William immediately recognised whose it was. He had admired this hair, its shade, for many months. It was a lock of Bessy Blake's hair, which John Stone had kept in his sales book. He had put it there knowing that he carried this with him everywhere he went, so there was a piece of his love that would be near to him every day. And when he was caught in the storm, he had pulled the book out, probably to look at the hair, knowing his life was soon to be lost. The thought of this stoked up jealousy in William's heart, jealousy which turned to anger. And he turned his back on the corpse to march away across the sand, back to his home. He had decided that the sea should take back the body of the soul it had claimed.

When word of what William had done, or not done, reached the people of Hoylake, they were all shaken. How could anyone do such an uncaring thing? Whatever rivalry there had been between the two men, surely William could see what his duty before God should be. He was accused of a selfish and callous act, and all who saw him from then on, old or young, shunned him. This was, however, the least of William's worries. To be scorned by Bessy was a far sharper cut to his heart. He had been jealous of John's favour with Bessy, but he could have been a support to the girl in her grief. His pitiless action had now removed him from all possible chances with Bessy. But as William wandered about the streets of Hoylake, thoughts of Bessy turned in his mind, like the waves of that fateful storm from the night before. Then faint images of the staring face of John Stone began to rise up before him. The image of those lifeless eyes in a white face, surrounded by black seaweed moving in the water, began to appear wherever he went. He saw that face staring out at him from the shadows, reflected in shop windows, and faintly watching him from the clouds above. William could feel his nerves failing him. He could not stand to see that face any more. He ran home, trying to block the image with his hands, half-closing his eyes, screaming. And those who saw him thought it was a madman running by.

William made it to his own house, where it appeared he was safe. That staring face did not appear again. Not until the night that is. When William went to bed, again his mind started to recall what he had seen, all he had heard and what he had experienced that day. He tossed and turned, and when he lay there, in his bed, on his back, from out of the darkness above him the face appeared again. John Stone was staring down at him, his white face bright in the night, surrounded by the black movement of seaweed about his head.

There was no escape for William, who screamed and screamed, covering his eyes to no avail. And there, hidden behind his hands, William's nerves failed him. His judgement had been served. William descended into a lifetime of shriek-filled madness.

And to all those who would listen, the shrimper said, 'If you fail to give a body found on the beach a good Christian burial, then the soul of that unfortunate will haunt you for the rest of your days.'

Twenty-seven

The Congleton Cannibal

There was once a widow who lived near Howty Brook, which connects Congleton to Astbury. Her name was Hannah Oakes and she lived in a tiny, tumbledown cottage. However, despite the small size of her dwelling, she would often have one particularly odd gentleman lodging there. Hannah needed the money and although he could be short-tempered and lungeous, she was happy to put up with his eccentricities if he paid his rent. His name was Samuel Thorley and although he had two jobs, he too had very little money. One of his jobs was as gravedigger, a lonely occupation which paid very little. The other was as a butcher, and it was said that he took such great delight in his work that he would often eat the meat raw. When he could no longer afford to pay for lodging at Hannah's cottage, he was often seen sleeping rough in the bushes alongside the brook. That was when it was fine. On wet nights, he would try to sleep in any barn about the place, but he was often caught and got into fights with the local farmers. Samuel had a short fuse, and the reputation of his temper went before him. What with upsetting the farmers, sleeping rough, having a temper and eating raw meat, Samuel found that he was not welcomed by many about the place. But Hannah didn't care, as long as he could pay.

It was on one evening, whilst Samuel was lodging at Hannah's cottage, that she cooked dinner for them both. Samuel was returned from work and burst in wearing his butcher's apron, carrying a hutchin of meat. Slapping it down on to the table, he demanded that Hannah cook it.

'Not tonight, Samuel. I've got dinner prepared already,' she replied.

The lodger was not happy and said she ought to cook this as well.

'I'm not starting on dinner again. What is it anyway?' she asked, as it looked like an unusual cut to her.

Samuel told her that it was a piece of pork which had been given to him by a pig farmer – someone he'd been doing some jobs for that afternoon.

Hannah looked at the meat and noticed it was wet. There was a damp patch developing on the wooden table.

'That's water from the brook,' Samuel hastily explained, 'I dropped the thing as I was coming up the path. I had to fish it out so I could bring it home. So you gonna cook it or not?'

Hannah explained again that she would not be cooking the meat, but if Samuel was so keen to have it, he was quite welcome to cook it himself once she had finished.

And that's what he did. Once Hannah had finished, Samuel took a big pan, filled it with water and began to boil the piece of meat. He didn't seem too interested in the dinner Hannah had cooked for them both, and she wasn't happy about that. However, she knew that with Samuel it was sometimes better to keep your mouth shut, so she went outside.

She had been out for about thirty minutes, when suddenly Samuel came rushing out, clutching his stomach. He then leant over one of the bushes and heaved, vomiting like a sick animal.

'Oh, for pity's sake, Samuel,' cried Hannah, 'what kind of beast are ya?'

Samuel wiped his mouth and, looking fairly green, he told Hannah to get rid of the meat. He wasn't going to be able to face it.

So Hannah went in, but it was a fairly large piece of pork and she was loath to throw it away. Money was tight and it wasn't unusual for poor folk in those days to make the most of any meat they found, even if it was rotten. So, she put it in a pan again to cook properly, and to remove all the fat which seemed good enough to eat.

As the water was slowly coming to the boil, she looked outside to see how Samuel was, but there was no trace of him. Instead, she noticed two finely dressed gentlemen walking down the pathway to her cottage.

'Good day to you,' called out one of them.

Hannah recognised him now. It was the local weaver, Thomas Cordwell. He introduced himself and the man who was with him, a Mr Thomas Elkin. Then he went on to ask if Samuel was about. Hannah had to answer that she had no idea where he had got to. Samuel had been about earlier, but since he was sick from some meat he had tried, he seemed to have gone missing.

The two men looked at each other and then Hannah noticed that Mr Elkin was wiping his hand with a handkerchief.

'Do you know anything about the bloodstains on the stile back there, Mrs Oakes?' asked Mr Cordwell.

'The stile at the end of my path there?' she asked, a little uncertain. 'No, I don't remember seeing any stains there. Bloodstains, you say?'

Then she rememberd, 'Oh, but Samuel just got back this afternoon with some meat, pork he said, which he had recently cut up. I's as reckon the blood will have dripped a bit from that, or his apron, as he crossed the stile to get to my cottage.'

'Would you mind if we saw this meat, Mrs Oakes?' asked Mr Elkin. 'If you still have it.'

'Oh, goodness!' gasped Hannah, 'Why, yes, it's boiling in the pan now. I need to check on it anyway.'

So, following the widow into the cottage, the two watched as she took the pan off the stove and lifted the lid. As the steam rose out, a smell hit their nostrils which created a strange feeling of disgust in their stomachs. Then, taking her tools, Hannah reached into the pan and pulled out the steaming meat.

Mr Elkin covered his mouth and nose, while Mr Cordwell pulled a face, but he looked closely. The two then glanced at each other before Mr Elkin signalled for Hannah to put the piece of meat back in the pan. Mr Cordwell replaced the lid and told Hannah to sit down.

He then began to tell her a tale which she did not expect, a tale about her lodger that meant she would never welcome Samuel Thorley back into her home again, no matter what he paid.

Two boys had been playing in the brook further up from Hannah's cottage earlier that day. Suddenly a blue cloak had come floating along. One of the boys, William, fetched it out with a stick and noticed that there were bloodstains on it. He and his friend were a bit uncertain about what to do, but working in the nearby field was the farmer, Newman Garside. So, the boys had gone to show him what they had found and, a little perturbed, Garside called over his farmhands. The three of them, and the two boys, went to the stream, just as another piece of clothing came floating along. This time it was a yellow blouse, also stained with blood. One of the farmhands had been taking a look along the bank for any clues as to what may have happened and stumbled across a small bag, which contained half a brown loaf and a sewing kit, as well as an old tobacco box. Searching through the undergrowth, they unearthed some song sheets and a woman's petticoat. There was then a cry from one of the farmhands, one who had remained at the brook. There, floating along through the water, was a severed human leg. He didn't want to touch it, but using a long branch lying on the bank, he managed to stop the leg floating past, and teased it over to the side where someone else could pick it up.

On seeing this, Garside sent the two boys off to fetch the local constable. It was looking like a murder of some sort had taken place there, and a grisly one at that. The search continued and various other parts of a woman were found, either floating in the brook or lying hidden in the bushes, having been thrown there by the murderer. Throughout the search there were various conversations over who the victim could be. Some thought that the fact that there were some song sheets, with the music for local ballads, meant it had to be someone associated with singing in the region. Others said that the song sheets were probably a red herring. The manuscript could've been dropped by someone else passing by at a different time. They all agreed, however, that it was a woman, the petticoat and the leg itself suggested this.

Finally, their questions were answered when an unfortunate fellow stumbled upon the severed head of the victim, lying in the depths of a bramblebush. It was the head of Anne Smith, the local ballad singer who was well known in all the pubs about the place, and equally well known to many of the local gentlemen.

So, with sadness, the pieces that had been found were taken and stored at a nearby barn, as the search continued for the other missing body parts. It was from here that Thomas Cordwell had decided, along with Thomas Elkin, to do some investigation himself. The pair returned to Howty Brook and followed the path until it brought them to a stile that led them to Hannah's cottage. And now here they were, telling the tale, having just seen a suspicious piece of meat.

Hannah sat back in her chair, feeling sick and unable to say a word.

'I must say, Mr Cordwell,' said Mr Elkin. 'That the piece of meat contained in that there pan, does look suspiciously like the calf muscle of a human leg.'

Hannah gasped.

'I agree, Mr Elkin. Might we take the specimen, Mrs Oakes, and put it together with the other remains of this poor, unfortunate woman?'

Hannah couldn't speak; she simply nodded with her hand over her mouth and waved with the other, as if to indicate that a quick removal of the specimen would be preferable.

This was the final piece of evidence that the community needed. At last, they not only had a reason to put away

Samuel Thorley, but, of course, the case of the cruel death of poor Anne Smith was solved. There was a lot of talk about the incident in all the pubs and market stalls around Congleton and Astbury. A number said how they had bought meat from Thorley in the past, and had thought that it tasted a bit odd. And so, all sorts of tales of the Congleton Cannibal began to spread about the region.

Samuel was found hiding in a barn along School Lane in Astbury and was immediately arrested. He was placed in the cells under Chester Castle, where judges only made an appearance twice a year. He spent almost six months in a damp, dark cell with just two beds, but often having to share with five other prisoners. Until, finally, Mr Justice Moreton arrived to rule on the case. Thorley made no real attempt to defend himself; he was found guilty and sentenced to death by hanging. It was reported that he 'showed no remorse for his crime and met his death with indifference'.

His body was brought to Priestly Fields, where it was placed in a gibbet and displayed for all to see. The boys of the local grammar school were given the afternoon off, so that they could go and view the local cannibal. No doubt the school masters hoped such a viewing would serve as a warning to all regarding the outcomes of laziness and avarice. And as he stood there, young William, the boy who had first found the blue cloak in Howty Brook, wondered whether Thorley had actually been the one who had killed poor Anne Smith. Or, had he simply found what he thought was pork meat on the path and, hoping to save some money, had brought it home? If so, then Anne's murderer was still free, somewhere around Congleton and Astbury. William shivered. It was safer to believe that Samuel Thorley was a cannibal and that the case was now closed.

Twenty-eight

The Headless Woman

Cheshire was thrown headlong into the English Civil War, being predominantly Royalist yet under the charge of the Parliamentarian commander, William Brereton. Almost every town and village has stories of atrocities committed in the name of the nation; I could probably fill a book with such tales. However, the story I am about to tell is one which shows how brutal this conflict became, and how its mark is still visible to this day. There are many versions of this story, with the horrendous act being executed in a number of possible sites in the area. I have therefore chosen my favourite of the tales, but all of them are intriguing and revealing.

Let us begin then in the midst of the Civil War. Prince Rupert had ridden through Cheshire causing all sorts of destruction, in that cavalier way of his. Meanwhile, the Parliamentarians took over stately homes and churches, hiding out behind the fortified walls and helping themselves to the treasures they found.

A band of Roundheads heard that the Royalist family of Hockenhull Hall, outside Tarvin, had vacated their home and, in their haste, they had left behind all their valuables. The soldiers did not want to miss such an opportunity and quickly raided the house in search of the family treasure. Although the house looked dark to them as they came riding up the drive, they soon found that the servants had remained. There was an initial skirmish, but the brave stand given by the household staff was no match for the determined soldiers. Therefore, the Parliamentarians were soon in the house and tearing through all its rooms and contents. Despite all the screams and threats, the Roundheads had soon gathered up what they thought was all the servants and started to grill them as to the whereabouts of the family silver and jewels. The staff, however, were too loyal to their master and would not reveal their hiding place. Some even said that the family had left with everything of value. Threats were made with pistols being pointed at the heads of the older members, but still the resilience of the servants remained.

Then, they all heard the screaming of a young woman as two soldiers stumbled into the room holding a servant girl they had found hiding in the basement. It was Dorothy Grace Trigg, who had only recently joined the household. The captain looked at his new prisoner and decided to push things further with his silent captives.

'Listen here, you disillusioned dolts,' he growled at the unwilling assembly, 'if you don't tell us where the family treasures are, then this girl is going to suffer. You may not tell us for the life of one of your elders, but this girl has her whole life ahead of her. You tell us or she loses her head.'

He gave a sharp command to the two men holding Dorothy, and they forced her to her knees. Then they pulled her arms out to the sides, so as to leave her neck more exposed. The captain unsheathed his sword and stood brandishing it as he eyed the servants standing there, each uncertain of what they should do.

Dorothy cried out to her colleagues to have mercy, to tell where the treasure was. She had no idea, only being a young servant girl and recently employed.

The servants felt great pity for her and could not stand to hear her cries and pleas. However, they were loyal to the family, their master and to the king. How could they help these traitors, even if Dorothy's life was in danger?

The captain gave them several chances to tell, but then he had to show that he was a man of his word. He placed the cold blade next to Dorothy's neck. She cried out again, pleading with those who were simply watching her. Then there was a whoosh as the captain pulled the sword back through the air, followed by a swift squelch and a thud. Blood splattered on to the clean white aprons of the serving women. Blood splattered on to the walls. Dorothy was dead.

The captain turned to face the servants again, wearing a grin that showed no remorse, only a cruel satisfaction that he had done what he had threatened. And now he wanted to know who would be next, or were they willing to tell? A few may have been ready to reveal the hiding place in that moment, if they had known it, but the next few minutes changed everything.

The captain heard a thud behind him. His own soldiers had let the body fall to the floor. This was not unusual, but it was then that he saw the servants' eyes grow wide. One screamed. One fainted. One fell to his knees, babbling away in frantic prayer. The captain spun round to see what was causing all this commotion. And there he saw Dorothy's body moving. Slowly, she was pushing herself up to awkwardly rise to her feet. Then, bent over, her two hands started searching about the floor, looking for the head which had moments ago been part of the body. Suddenly, it was as if she was aware of the soldiers, who stood dumbfounded. She gave an abrupt lunge towards them. The lack of eyes meant her hands simply clawed at the air, but the Roundheads did not wait about for a second attack. Screaming half-remembered Biblical phrases and cursing the headless woman, they bolted from the room and out of the house, leaving the servants to watch the diabolical scene.

Dorothy's body then returned to its search for her head. It was lying against the wall a yard or two away, the back of it facing the servants.

'It's after the head,' screamed the housekeeper, 'Give it the head! Someone give it the head!'

No one wanted to get near the stumbling decapitated servant girl; neither did they want to touch her severed head. Yet the body stumbled about so much and turned towards the petrified huddle so many times in its search that, in the end, the old butler leant forward with his stick and tapped the head with his arm extended. His intention was to flip it across the floor to the body, but he only succeeded in flipping it around. There were screams, further faintings and more prayers as two eyes stared out of the head, two eyes that seemed to be alive in some demonic manner – searching about, looking for the body.

Then the butler gave out a yell, as a hand grabbed his arm. That animated body, so desperate to be reunited with the head, grasped at whatever came near. The butler wrenched himself free and, in fear more than callousness, slid his foot across the floor to kick the head to the feet of the searching body. As soon as foot and head connected, the hands reached down and picked up their missing member. Cradling her head as a mother with a child, the body stood up straight again. In placing the head under the left arm, it was as if its sight had been restored. The eyes of the speechless face glared at the butler, but his clumsy action had brought head and body back together, and so it seemed the undead form of Dorothy Trigg begrudgingly allowed him some gratitude. Then, seeing all those before her staring with dread, she strode towards the window with awkward confidence, smashed the glass with her fist, again to gasps and screams, and clambered out into the night.

It is said then that she wandered all about the grounds of Hockenhull Hall, then out into the surroundings. She traipsed over the Hockenhull Platts and eventually found herself on the main Chester Road. Here she wandered aimlessly, a pitiful half-conscious soul, looking for rest but stuck in the world of the living. Of course, sightings of this headless woman were recorded and she is still seen to this day. Some tell of how

they have seen her crossing the Platts, wandering over those crossings in the evening mist. Others have seen her walking along the Chester Road, near to the pub which bears her name. And some say she has wandered down even as far as Peckforton Castle, where they have seen her walking along the path which crosses the Haunted Bridge. Dorothy Grace Trigg, the poor headless woman, remains a key figure in the folklore of this part of Cheshire between Tarvin and Peckforton, and it seems that she has no intention of being forgotten.

Twenty-nine

Good Hearty Lads

The ringing of a bell was a constant sound in the life of working folk some hundred or so years ago. Church bells would call the people to the Sunday service, or at least tell the workers to come in from the fields to take the Eucharist. Bells were rung in school for the beginning and end of lessons – as they still are in many schools. Bells marked the beginning and end of work. Bells rang out from cash registers, from over the opening doors of shops, and to summon staff. Finally, the church bell would be rung at a funeral, the death knell. No wonder then, when it was dark and quiet, that folk would think they could hear a mysterious bell ringing somewhere in the distance. This may, partly, be the origin for stories like the 'Mermaid of Rostherne Mere'.

There is tell of a bell which sometimes peals out from under Wildboarclough Hills, in the far east of Cheshire, where our flat county rises up to meet the Peak District. This desolate village on the steep winding road also once hosted a Pancake Tuesday Hen Fair, the high point of which was a competition in which a hen was the prize. Competitors would have to stand back from a bobbin, and then throw long sticks at the tiny target. The closest to the bobbin would win a hen. And the winner for many years was from nearby Oven Farm, a man named Old Tom Barlow, who claimed that he never had to fork out money for a hen, such were his superior throwing skills. But in *The Shiny Night,* Beatrice Tunstall mentions how at one of the nearby meres a more sombre event took place. A Black Souler, from the local souling gang, lost his way and in the darkness of the night tripped and fell into a water pit. He lost his life, but his soul remains in the depths of the mere. On a quiet night you can hear the sound of his bell, its ringing echoing up to those who pass by. Is it a warning to keep clear of the mere? Or is it a warning that he may rise up to meet whoever is passing? Few stay around long enough to find out.

Souling refers to a sight which was fairly common each year around Cheshire, when October meets November. This is the time of All Saints' Day or All Souls' Day, the night before being 31 October and known as All Hallows' Eve (which is, of course, Halloween). The traditions of 'Trick or Treat' have spread across the world and have become the main ritual on Halloween for children in almost every part of the country. Sadly, it has taken over the more local traditions celebrating those curious two days. It has also become the domain of children, which seems to happen to many of our cultural or religious ceremonies in Europe. Yet, before the Irish-American invasion of Halloween, it was grown men who would dress up and take to the streets. They would certainly visit the local pubs but also the houses, bringing with them the local tradition of souling. Boys would also knock on doors and beg for sweet things, such as fruit and soulcakes, while singing the Soulcake Song.

Soul! Soul! For a soul cake.
I pray, good missis, a soul cake,
An apple, or pear, a plum or a cherry,
Any good thing to make us merry …

The flat soulcakes (spiced biscuity circles), would be piled high, ready for handing out to the boys as they came by. But the men would be out and about as well, being a gang of soulers, after something more liquid than soulcakes and parading from pub to pub with their Souling Plays. These plays would vary from village to village, but generally followed the same pattern. The gang would also be known to visit some of the larger houses in the area, where they would receive some payment. It is thought that this was to ensure the gang would move on fairly quickly.

Dressed as an array of characters, their variations being tied to the local traditions, at least one member of the gang would blacken his face – the Black Souler. Although, this name seems not to have been for any one of the characters, but more of a general term for the one who is blackened up. He might be known then as the Letter-In or the character Belcher Bob. The black on his face was there to hide his features and so keep some mystery about the proceedings.

And so first, in comes … let's say it's Belcher Bob, whose name derives from Beelzebub. In he comes carrying a dripping pan which clangs as he hits it with his club, with a ring-ting-ting. He makes sure he has the full attention of those in the pub, being a bit surly and looking like a ruffian off the street. His coat is tied about his waist with string and he may even have a clog hanging over one shoulder. But once all are aware that the play is about to begin, the real action starts.

In comes King George, who has returned from his great adventures. He carries a sword in his hand and is dressed like a soldier from Victorian times. He boasts of how he slew the dragon and so rescued the King of Egypt's daughter. He was given her hand in marriage and a bag of gold. Puffed up and full of himself, George parades about the pub showing off his uniform and his weaponry.

In comes George's nemesis. This is a blackened-faced warrior who can be known as Turkey Snipe or Prince Paradise. He arrives in his armour and may have a plume of feathers bursting from his helmet. He too brandishes a sword and tells the crowd how he has come to take on the arrogant King George.

King George is not one to turn down a challenge and, vowing to make his enemy into mince pies, a fierce fight begins. There in the pub, the two are locked in mortal combat. It is often George who is cheered on by the locals, who are careful to ensure their drinks don't get knocked over. Those two warriors swing their swords this way and that – the clacking of wood sounding out when the weapons meet. Staggering back here and there, the battle careers around the pubs until, suddenly, King George attains a moment's advantage. He is not slow and strikes his enemy with a mortal blow. The blackened man clasps his side and cries out. Falling to the ground as dramatically as he can, with the sword still stuck in his side, he is dead. King George then turns to the crowd to receive their raucous adulation.

In comes a man dressed as a woman. This is the defeated warrior's mother. Grief-stricken, she runs to her son and kneels at his side. She tells all watching how this is her one and only child. How cruel war is, that she should have her son taken from her. Who will look after her now?

King George is a little taken aback by the appearance of the mother. It seems he only saw that there was a duel to be had. He had no thought that his enemy should have a mother. Together, King George and Belcher Bob lead the call for a doctor, which is often accompanied by some quacking.

In comes the Quack Doctor, sometimes called Doctor Brown. He is carrying a bag and wears a long, black coat and a top hat. He tells the people about how he has travelled far and wide. He tells them of all the strange things that he has seen, including houses made of food, such as pork pies and sausages. He talks of pigs that run around with knives and forks stuck in their backs, until he sees the weeping old woman. Then he reaches into his bag and pulls out a bottle. He shoves the bottle on to the dead son's lips, making him drink with a thrittle throttle. The crowd and the mother wait to see if the Quack Doctor's remedy will work. Then the warrior jolts. He jumps up. He is alive! A cheer rises from the crowd and the old woman is overjoyed. But he is holding his back. It seems that even though he is alive, he is not totally cured. No matter, his mother is pleased to have him back and she will take care of him.

Then in come a number of other characters. In some regions it is now Beelzebub, for others it is Dairy Doubt or Jerry Doubt, who can also be dressed as some kind of Devil. It could even be Jolly Jack Tar, or an intriguingly silent fellow known as Pigtail. Wearing a pig mask, this character does not speak but makes his presence clear by bashing a tambourine. He has a particular use for this which comes into play a little later, but first …

In comes Dick with his driver. This is the highlight of a souling play, with Dick being the name of the hoden horse. The word 'hoden' rhymes with 'wooden' and the tradition of the hoden horse is found all over England, often being associated with morris dancing or mummery. The Cheshire version is often made using a horse's skull, which can be painted black with bulging eyes attached. After all, it is said by his driver, 'He was alive, but now he's dead'. Some gangs do not use a skull, but make a horse's head out of two broom heads fixed together. Either way, his mouth needs to open and close for the full effect. The hoden horse is operated by a man wrapped in a blanket, to hide both himself and the broomstick to which the horse's head is attached. He is brought into the fray and gallops about the room visiting the onlookers, the horse's mouth opening and closing, the clacking sound of its teeth making a distinctive and slightly unnerving sound about the pub. Whilst this is going on, the Driver tells of Dick's adventures. He was pulling a cart of firbobs all the way from Mouldsworth, when they went over a bump and one of the bobs fell from the cart and hit his leg. Dick kicked back in such a frenzy that the cart was completely destroyed. That may explain why he only has three legs. So, the Driver plays on the sympathies of the crowd to raise some money, said to pay for more beer. This is where Pigtail will come forward to take up his speechless but important role. His tambourine now upturned, he goes through the crowd rattling his improvised collecting bowl. Of course, nowadays the money is given to local charities, as the landlord will often stand the gang a pint each.

And so, the gang finally come together and break into song. There are many versions of souling songs across the county, but

this verse from the Stapleford play gives a good flavour of the spirit of souling, I believe.

We are one, two, three good hearty lads,
We are all in one mind.
We have all come a souling good nature to find.
And if you will give us one jug of your beer,
We will not come a-souling
Till this time next year.

With the song sung and the beer all downed, the soulers leave the pub to go on to the next, where they again perform their play. And then on to the next. And maybe even the next. It is not surprising then, that sometime in the history of souling, one blackened-faced souler finally lost his footing and ended up in a nearby mere, bell and all.

Thirty

The Cat o'Nine Tales

When I was planning to return to England, having lived abroad for a number of years, I was amazed at how many of my international friends had heard of Cheshire, but for one thing only – the Cheshire Cat. Lewis Carroll's book *Alice's Adventures in Wonderland* is certainly known worldwide, and has put the county in people's minds, if not quite 'on the map'. I had to explain many times where Cheshire actually is. However, as to the origins of the fabled cat, nobody is quite sure, and each explanation I have heard makes quite a tale in itself. Lewis Carroll, whose real name was Charles Dodgson, a Cheshire man, spent his childhood in Daresbury. His presence remains, celebrated in a dramatic window at the village's All Saints' Church. Commissioned in 1932 to celebrate the author's centenary, it was finally dedicated three years later, and shows the Nativity of Christ, with Carroll kneeling at the crib and Alice standing beside him. A host of Wonderland characters take their place along the bottom of each of the window's panels. The Cheshire Cat is there too, with his distinctive smile, and so begins my exploration of this enigmatic creature's origins.

Carroll visited many places across the country, but spent his adult life at Oxford. Towns as far flung as Llandudno, Guildford and Beverley therefore all make a claim to the author and his Cheshire Cat, often citing an unusual carving in a local church as the inspiration for the beast.

Stony Looks

There are two churches in Cheshire that purport to having the inspiration for the cat. One is St Wilfrid's at Grappenhall, which is only 5 miles away from Daresbury. The cat is a well-known feature on the walls of the church, stretching out along the building with its face turned so that all can see its wide grin – from ear to ear. It's thought that the young Lewis Carroll would have seen the cat, if he happened to visit the church and look above the west window. But, you may be wondering why a cat appears in the church masonry at all. It is believed that this image relates to the owner of Caterich, a house in the parish owned by Robert De Boydell, of Catterick. This property, with an impressive moat, is bounded by the road named Cartridge Lane. It is thought that this was once named Caterich Lane, but over the years Caterich has been corrupted to Cartridge. There would, therefore, have been two 'cats' in the area, which may have helped to prompt the young Carroll's imagination. It is also interesting to note that an early ancestor of Robert de Boydell, Sir William, has an effigy inside St Wilfrid's Church, which sports a surprising smile. Is Sir William, in fact, the original grinning Cheshire Cat?

Almost 30 miles away, at Pott Shrigley, outside of Macclesfield, there is another church that also makes the claim for the Cheshire Cat. It is said that Dodgson visited this church and saw the unusual carving of a cat's head in the chancel. The cat at St Christopher's does look remarkably similar to the pictures by John Tenniel, and Carroll is known to have been quite pernickety about the illustrations for his books.

All these features sound fairly plausible as being contenders for the original inspiration for the Cheshire Cat, but there is just one problem. The phrase 'to grin like a Cheshire cat' predates *Alice's Adventures in Wonderland* by almost 200 years. These church sculptures, together with the Caterich house, may have inspired Carroll, but it seems that he only popularised the idea of the Cheshire Cat rather than created it. Reference is often made to John Wolcot, who wrote under the pen-name of Peter Pindar. In his *Pair of Lyric Epistles* we find the phrase, 'Lo! Like a Cheshire Cat our court will grin'. But there are others. There is the rather grating idea of 'grinning like a Cheshire cat chewing gravel' and the more pleasant, 'to grin like a Cheshire cat eating cheese'. As these phrases came along centuries before Lewis Carroll, how else could the idea of a smiling cat from Cheshire have arisen?

MILKY LOOKS

The Cheshire Plain stretches out like the base of a frying pan. The rich land is perfect for dairy farming, so it is no wonder that the county is well known across the country for its production of both milk and cheese. With cats being useful on a farm, it's not difficult to imagine that the cats of Cheshire would be the happiest felines in the country, surrounded by all that milk. And so the phrase 'to grin like a Cheshire cat' could make a lot of sense.

With so much milk in Cheshire, the locals would try out many other ways of using the nutritious liquid, and numerous milk-based puddings have been tried and developed over the years. One story tells of how the people of Bunbury would make a large milk pudding every year for their village Wakes. It may have been frumenty, which was a popular dish for Wakes, being made primarily from grain, milk and eggs. Milk would be collected from all the farms around and stored at Tiverton Hall Farm, with each dairy farmer being part of the great project. Now, it happened that, one year, the farmer in charge of storing the milk noticed that some of it had gone missing. When he lifted the lid, he noticed that the churn was a lot less full than it should have been, and the more churns he opened, the more milk he found to be missing. The Bunbury Pudding was well known in the area and known for its size. This mysterious loss of milk would jeopardise the pudding this year, making it a poorer cousin when compared to those of past Wakes. And so, the farmer set off to investigate.

He asked the workers and searched about the farm, but he found no clues. Not until he happened to watch the cats, who were acting quite strangely. Every so often, one or two would head off out of the farm and on to the lane, but they did not come back. They were soon followed by others and so it went on. Curious at this sight, the farmer decided that he would follow too. He walked up the lane, which lead to Huxley, but saw the cats heading off down a track, the one that joins up with Crib Lane. Here he saw clowders of cats coming from the other farms, pushing through the bushes, leaping over walls, crawling under fences and tripping down the lane meowing, with their tails held high. The farmer could not help but follow and found the furry troop leading him to one of his workers' cottages. The cats were all scurrying around the back, where the door had been left ajar. Stepping over the feline interlopers, the farmer cautiously pushed the door open and tiptoed in. There seemed to be no one in the cottage, it was empty but for the constant flowing crowd of cats. Pushing his way through, the farmer followed to where they all seemed to be heading, which was up the stairs and into the bedroom. There the room was full of cats all clambering over a chest of drawers, which had a couple of its drawers open. Pushing the mewing burglars out of the way, the farmer discovered the spoils of the real thief. In the drawers were jugs and pots and bowls, all full of milk. He pulled open other drawers and found more containers filled to the brim. He had uncovered the full stash of stolen milk. So, before the smiling Cheshire cats could lap up any more, he put the lids back on, shut the drawers and shooed the moggies out of the house. Then he closed the back door and ran back to Tiverton Hall to fetch a band of workers to help him move it all back to the farm. They all knew whose cottage that was, and funnily enough that particular worker was nowhere to be seen that day.

Having emptied the milk into a few churns and loaded the wagon, the workers headed off back to Tiverton Hall down the track. They laughed to think of their friend's audacity and how he would now be the least popular man in the parish. 'Ha ha, who would've thought that he would've stashed all the milk for the pudding!' said one.

'Aye, and no one's ever gonna forget that!'

'No, from now on this track'll be known as Pudding Road or Milky Track, I as reckon.'

'Ha-ha,' laughed another, 'yeah, Pudding Lane sounds good to me.'

And from that day on the track became known as Pudding Lane which it is to this day, a lane joining Crib Lane and Huxley Lane there behind Tiverton Hall Farm.

Cheesy Smiles

The Cheshire mon ran to his hold,
And fetched a Cheshire Cheese;
And said, 'Look here you dog! Behold
We had such fruits as these!
Your fruits are ripe but twice a year,

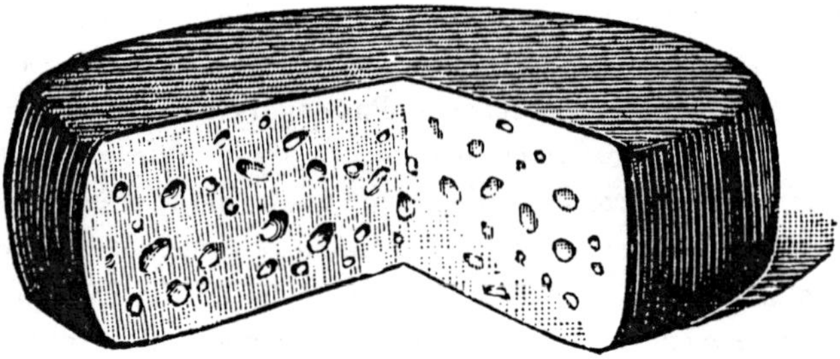

As you yourself did say;
But such as I present you here
Our land brings twice a day.'

From 'The Cheshire Cheese', a folk song first published in 1745.

I've already mentioned the abundance of milk in Cheshire, and hinted at the prolific cheese manufacturing and, of course, there is the phrase, 'to grin like a Cheshire Cat eating cheese'. So, it is not surprising that there is one story suggested for the origins of the happy feline that relates to the cheese industry. There was a time when cheese-making was so widespread in Cheshire that almost every farm made its own. With every farm having its own idiosyncrasies, each would produce something with a unique flavour (some more palatable than others, I am sure). Such a basic commodity would at least keep the household fed, and many of these cheeses would have gone on to be sold at the markets in the towns around Cheshire. In fact, Cheshire Cheese is said to be the oldest known British cheese, and is described in the *Foodie Handbook* as having 'a savoury, mellow and slightly salty taste with a loose, crumbly texture'. Daniel Defoe in his book *A Tour Through the Whole Island of Great Britain*, said that the Cheshire cheese was also found in Shropshire, Staffordshire and Lancashire and 'was shipped by river all over the country in enormous quantities, 14,000 tons a year going to London alone'. A pretty famous cheese then, so renowned, in fact, that when the famous Tom Thumb (Charles Sherwood Stratton) came through the county on his tour of England and Wales, it is said that he allowed himself to be carried in to dinner whilst sitting cross-legged on a Cheshire round. The cheese seems not to have been to everyone's taste, however, as Henry Fielding shows in his play *The Life and Death of Tom Thumb the Great.*

> Long may they live, and love, and propagate,
> Till the whole land be peopled with Tom Thumbs!
> So, when the Cheshire cheese a maggot breeds,
> Another and another still succeeds:
> By thousands and ten thousands they increase,
> Till one continued maggot fills the rotten cheese.

The character speaking was actually a Welsh parson, and long has there been rivalry between the people of Cheshire and those across the border. Still, the parson may also be referring to a method of making cheese, which is used for the Sardinian casu marzu, which translates as 'rotten cheese'; also known as the 'maggot cheese'. It is made with the larvae of the cheese fly and pecorino sardo (a hard cheese). The maggots feed on the cheese, causing it to decompose, thus giving it a soft, runny consistency with a pungent aroma. They say you best eat it with the maggots still in and still alive, so it is not surprising to hear that such a cheese is banned across the world. Although Fielding's parson connects this method with the Cheshire cheese, I have found no evidence of the practice in this county, or anywhere hereabouts.

There are no maggots to be found in Cheshire cheese. So proud were the local farmers of their produce that they wanted to find a way to make their cheese distinctive from their competitors. They wanted people to know it was a Cheshire cheese when they saw it. Now, the sign of Cheshire has always been the lion, and so a cheese in the shape of the king of the beasts was seen as a fitting way to distinguish it from those others down London way. Very soon new cheese moulds were made, quite incredible things, that would present the cheese as a lion; and how proud the cheese-makers were – until the cheeses went to market.

'What's that cat cheese?' piped up one voice from the crowd.

'Where?' asked another.

'There. A funny thing with a sickly grin on its face!'

One of the Cheshire men quickly stepped forward, 'We'll have you know, Sir, that this is the fine Cheshire cheese shaped as our majestic lion, if you like.'

The gathering crowd laughed. 'Lion?' said one, 'Grinning cat, more like.'

The Cheshire mon was not going to be put off by a Londoner, 'What you call a grin, Sir, is in fact the sharp teeth being shown. Our proud beast growls at all other cheeses, especially those that call themselves Cheshire, but come from the likes of Staffordshire and Shropshire.'

Yet the crowd simply laughed at him, for as the poor Cheshire mon tried to convince them of the leonine design, one playful marketeer had come up behind him with a handful of straw and poked pieces of it into the lion's cheeks, making long cat-like whiskers.

'Look at that then, mates,' he chuckled, 'it's the noble cat from Cheshire.'

The Cheshire mon could do nothing to dissuade the laughter, and soon was competing against calls of 'Here, Puss-Puss!' and 'Who wants to pet the Cheshire Cat?'

And so the gossip rattled about the market place and very soon folk were talking about the grinning Cheshire Cat, a tale they took back home, and a new phrase entered the English language.

Mistaken Looks

This confusion over a growling lion comes up again as an alternative explanation for the Cheshire Cat. Lions have appeared regularly in heraldic designs and the first Earl of Chester was no exception. However, very few people in mediaeval England had ever seen a lion. They had to paint the creature based on people's descriptions, and so all sorts of strange-looking animals appeared at this time, many of which looked like they had the face of a man. The growling teeth better resembled a grimace, while the face was draped in long hair, and sitting atop the body of a cat. And so, the Earl of Chester's coat of arms was said to have a cat, and this became known as the Cheshire Cat.

Even if you have seen a lion, drawing such a creature may be as difficult as sketching a horse, getting the proportions of the body right, making sure the head is not too small or too large. And so, as many public houses were named after lions throughout the county, so a proliferation of badly drawn beasts appeared hanging on almost every main street of every market town. There were Red Lions and White Lions, and Gold Lions and Black Lions, and even a Blue Lion. So, with folk coming in from the countryside and from other counties, it soon became a comical sight to recount, and the idea of the smiling Cheshire Cat spread far and wide.

There are a number of pubs with intriguing names about the county. The Wizard at Nether Alderley clearly refers to the tale of the Wizard of Alderley Edge, and there are a number of Royal Oaks said to be in honour of Charles I's hiding place. Two found on the A49 with interesting names include Cabbage Hall and the Fox & Barrel. Apparently, tailors in the past used to collect together the off-cuts from material used to make suits commissioned by customers. These off-cuts would be used to make a little more money, as clothes could be made for other customers, for which the tailor did not have to purchase any more material. This procedure is known as 'cabbaging'. One tailor did this for so long that he was eventually able to finance a change of career. He bought a pub and set himself up as a landlord. In memory of the way in which he raised the finances, he named the tavern Cabbage Hall.

Further south on the A49 there is the Fox & Barrel, which is said to be named after an early hunt saboteur. The landlord was overseeing the delivery of ales to his pub, then called the King's Head. He could hear the Cheshire hunt, the sound of horn and hounds thundering over the fields. Then, in search of somewhere to hide, a panicked fox dashed out from the bushes and across the road. It dived through the cellar doors and scuttled down behind the barrels. The landlord could hear the hunt was on its way, the barking getting ever closer. He had to admit that he didn't really like those jumped-up gentry types, so quickly he closed the cellar doors and waited. Very soon the horses clattered on to the road with the dogs sniffing about the pub. The head of the hunt looked down at the landlord and called out, 'Seen the fox about, my man?'

'Aye,' answered the landlord slowly, 'he went bolting off that way.' And he pointed off to the fields on the other side of the pub.

Thanking him, the red-coated man shouted the news to the others on the hunt, and gathering the dogs they set off into the neighbouring fields.

The landlord waited a bit until the hunt sounded to be a good way off and then he opened the cellar doors. Looking inside he saw old Reynard sat up on one of the barrels.

'You needn't look so pleased with yourself,' said the landlord, 'if it wasn't for me, those dogs would've been sniffing all about here and waiting for you outside.'

With that the fox jumped down to the floor and scampered up the steps into the daylight. With a brief look back to the landlord, he was off, back to the field he had come from, knowing that the hunt were a long way off in the other direction.

And from then on, the pub became known as the Fox & Barrel.

Hungry Looks

When thinking about shipping in the north-west of England, many immediately mention Liverpool, which was known as the gateway to the British Empire. However, Chester was once the busiest port in the north-west, before it had issues with silt. From Roman times to the eighteenth century, Chester had a bustling harbour with vessels travelling to Scotland, Ireland and parts of mainland Europe. During the Middle Ages it was the most prosperous port in the whole of Britain.

Now with all those ships coming in from lands afar, and closer to home, the cats of Chester knew that if they were hungry, all they had to do was make their way to the harbour and await a ship. Whatever cargo the ship would have it would also be guaranteed to be carrying rats. Rats from all over the world – what an exotic menu.

Sailors coming into England would talk about the cats of Cheshire and look out for them. As their vessel drew into the harbour, they would see the cats sitting along the jetty, waiting for them to dock.

'See the Cheshire cats waiting for us,' they'd say, 'they know what's hidden aboard this ship and they'll soon be here.'

'Aye, look at them. They know they're gonna get a slap-up meal very soon.'

'And what a grin is on the face of each one of them.'

And so the phrase grinning like a Cheshire cat became a favourite amongst the sailors, seafarers who were from all across Great Britain, and their families who would listen to their stories. The Cheshire Cat then became a popular idea with the seafaring families of Britain, wherever they lived.

Or was it not the feline cats that stood on the ports waiting for the ships with big grins, but the human ones? The women also waited on the harbour-side with wide, toothy grins to welcome home the men who had missed female company for weeks or for months. Some have said that as charming as the cats awaiting rats story is, it was another set of 'cats' on the dockside that gave birth to the phrase 'grinning like a Cheshire cat'.

HAPPY SMILES

The following is a story which is hard to verify. It is one I have only heard from a tiny number of sources, but it is one of my favourites and reminds me also of a colourful local character named Maggoty Johnson. His real name was Samuel Johnson, although he was not a doctor but a jester. I have already mentioned the maggoty cheese in my tales, but for Johnson the maggoty is a joke about his character, being a Cheshire euphemism for madness. Maggoty Johnson was in fact a dancing master at Gawsworth Hall, but like many of the colourful characters involved in the arts, he liked to try to spread his influence into other disciplines and wrote a play for which he played the lead role of Lord Flame. He enjoyed such plaudits that it went to his head and from then on he expected everyone to address him as 'My Lord Flame'. I expect that such behavior only helped to seal his maggoty reputation. Despite this, he must have been a beloved member of the Gawsworth Hall household as when he died in 1773, aged eighty-two, he was buried in the grounds and his grave is there to this day. But he was not so well loved by all, it may seem, from a later inscription on his gravestone which runs as follows:

If chance hath brought thee here, or curious eyes,
To see the spot where this poor jester lies,
A thoughtless jester even in his death,
Uttering his jibes beyond his latest breath,
O stranger pause a moment, pause and say:
'Tomorrow should'st thou quit thy house of clay,
Where wilt thou be my soul? in Paradise?
Or where the rich man lifted up his eyes.'
Immortal spirit would'st thou then be blest,
Waiting thy perfect bliss on Abraham's breast,
Boast not of silly art or wit or fame,
Be thou ambitious of a Christian's name,
Seek not thy body's rest in peaceful grove,
Pray that thy soul may rest in Jesus' love,
O speak not lightly of that dreadful day,
When all must rise in joy or dismay.
When spirits pure in body glorified,
With Christ in Heavenly mansions shall abide,
While wicked souls shall hear the Judge's boom,
'Go ye accursed into endless gloom,'
Look on that stone and this, and ponder well,

Then choose twixt Life and Death,
Heaven and Hell.

With such sombre words, it might be better now to consider someone who could bring a smile to the face and so birth the phrase 'to grin like a Cheshire Cat'.

It was long ago when one of the Earls of Chester, like many of his day, had a court jester. A man of many talents and quick wit who was called Cat Caitlin. Now Mr Caitlin had the favour of his master and was not only light on his feet and fast with his tongue. He was also clever enough to speak the truth whilst appearing to be a fool and so made many of the Earl's court laugh and smile. In fact, his insights and way with words were so endearing that even when he had left the room, his audience would still be grinning, unable to stop thinking about the witty lines Cat Caitlin had delivered.

It was when the Earl of Chester was showing off his jester to a visiting dignitary up from London that an idea was considered. The respected guest was so taken with the entertainments and the humour of Mr Caitlin that he asked whether the jester could accompany him when he returned to London. 'There are many in the capital who would find this man of yours so amusing,' he told the Earl, 'and of course I will say he is your jester and this will put you in a very good light amongst the gentry of the city, many of whom I am sure would wish to form a connection with you.'

Now it was most unusual that a jester should be allowed to visit other households, but the Earl was so proud of Cat Caitlin and impressed by his guest's words that he granted permission for his man to go on this trip and remain in London for a limited amount of time.

And so, Cat Caitlin packed his bags and joined the dignitary to journey to the capital. On the way there, the jester entertained the hosts of the houses which they stayed at overnight. He was received with such delight and created such hilarity that by the time he reached London, word of him had already swept the

city and many came to see this Cat Caitlin of Cheshire for themselves.

None was disappointed and for some months the gentry of London were entertained. Always when Cat Caitlin left the room, a smile remained on the faces of his audience, who continued their evening in the most jovial of moods.

The respected guest was right, word of the Earl did spread, as did the jokes and tricks of his jester, until it was time for Mr Caitlin to return to his master. Again, he travelled back through England but this time stopping off at the inns along the way, where he again entertained his hosts. Cat's humour was so keen that he could bring laughter to all of England's people, whatever their station. It was on this journey that he received many a free meal and much ale and I daresay added a few inches to his girth, till he was welcomed back to Chester where the Earl and his court enjoyed again the fun and laughter of their own, now illustrious, jester.

And back in London, the gentry remembered him. As well as in the grand houses and the inns throughout England.

Even though he was no longer with them his jokes remained in the shared memory of those people, who would often recall the day that the jester came.

'What was his name again?' someone would ask.

'I believe it was Cat,' someone would answer.

'Not our cat then,' someone would joke.

'No, the jester from Chester.'

'Ah yes, that Cheshire Cat.'

And a smile would appear again on the faces of all who remembered. Even though he was long gone, the smile of that Cheshire cat remained. And so it was often said, 'Lo! Like a Cheshire cat our court will grin.'

False Smiles

In my years of gathering Cheshire lore, I found it curiously odd that in the old dialect a 'grin' refers to a snare. This usually means one set for a hare or a rabbit, but think of those larger traps set for bears or even for men. A trap like this, when it is shut, could certainly be described as a 'grin', as the sharp teeth come together like a vicious mouth.

Poachers, of which there were many in Cheshire, would need to be careful of traps such as these. If such a trap caught a man's leg, he would look down to see a sickly, wide, cat-like grin smiling up at him, gloating at his pain. Could the phrase 'to grin like a Cheshire cat' refer more to a trap?

Sleepy Smiles

It has been suggested that the Cheshire Cat is a reference to a distinctive British feline, the British blue shorthair. This is a small, stocky breed, which has a distinctive smile. A number of adaptations of *Alice's Adventures in Wonderland* for film and television have shown the Cheshire Cat as being grey.

Whether it was the early Celtic Cornovii, the Saxons or the Vikings, there seem to have always been people in what is now Cheshire bringing with them their cats. The Cornovii have even been known as the people of the cat. The Saxons would ensure in a divorce that the man kept at least one of the household's cats, whilst his wife could keep the rest. And for a hamlet to have legal status on the Welsh borders it would have to contain one feline. It's possible then that all this cat lore helped found Cheshire traditions, being added to by the growing local customs and merging with the landscape.

The Viking story of Cat Bayun catches my attention in the search for the Cheshire Cat. This mysterious character appears in collections of Russian fairytales, but I include the story here as it is possible that Ingimund's Norsemen and the Danes of the time knew of this cat, and their descendants held it in mind so that this idea became part of the development of the idea of the Cheshire Cat.

Thor had come down the Rainbow Bridge from Asgard to Midgard early one morning to do some fishing. He was standing on the riverbank of the Mersey throwing his large net into the river, hoping to catch a dragon that was said to swim in its waters. This may have been the Moston Dragon, before it had moved to Bache Pool where it was later slain by Sir Thomas Venables. Or it may have been one of its cousins. We are not sure which it was, but Thor was out fishing for a dragon, as he needed to bring a gift back to Asgard for the goddess Freya. He was not sure if she would really welcome a dragon, but it was all he knew how to catch and Thor felt it would show how brave and strong he was. 'Freya will be impressed at such a gift,' he thought, 'or will she?'

After a while Thor began to tire, so he pulled in the net and decided to sit for a while. Would a dragon be the best gift for Freya? He had to admit he was not entirely convinced. And as he sat there, Thor was a little confused at something else. He, the great Viking God of Thunder, rarely grew tired and it was not as if he was fighting a battle. He had simply been throwing a net into the water and dragging it back.

Certainly it was heavy when wet, but Thor was surprised that such a task should take so much strength out of him.

Sat on the bank, he stretched his arms and yawned, feeling a sleepiness clouding over his eyes and making his head heavy. And as his head gently nodded forward, Thor became aware of a tune, which he could faintly hear behind him. A beautiful male voice was wafting over the Plain and lulling him to sleep. Thor wasn't sure he liked being put to sleep in this way, but the sweet light voice had weakened him and he was not convinced he could even stand, let alone resist the charms of this lullaby. And as Thor began to snore, the song became quieter and quieter and then stopped – the God of Thunder snoozing happily on the riverbank.

Suddenly, he was rudely awoken. A great high-pitched wailing now rang out over the Plain. Thor jumped up and clamped his hands over his ears. Looking about in disdain, he saw a small wood not so far away. As he could see no one else about he decided the screaming and the singing must have been coming from there. Picking up his mighty hammer, mjolnir, Thor strode over to the trees, despite the ear-piercing squeals that grew louder with every step. Then the singing arose again and the screaming sounds grew quieter and quieter. Now Thor had to resist the soporific effects of that voice instead of the head-splitting cries, but his determination saw him striding into those woods. Defiantly scanning about the trees, he spied a long, hairy tail hanging down from the leaf-covered branch of an old oak tree. That must be where the singer is, he thought, and stamped through the fallen leaves and twigs to see who was making these noises of such extremes. As he came closer, a furry grey head suddenly dropped down from the branch. It was a cat, poking its head out from the leaves, with a paw pressed to its mouth, telling Thor to hush.

The Thunder God was so taken aback, he immediately obeyed and walked more carefully, ensuring that he cracked no twig and rustled the leaves as little as possible. That great warrior god tiptoed up to the tree and saw at its foot the focus of the cat's concern. Curled up in the leaves, between two great roots, slept two blue kittens, their snores nothing more than tiny mewing sounds.

'Are you the one who has been singing and screaming?' Thor asked the adult cat in a whisper.

The grey and black striped creature smiled a broad grin. 'I am the one who sings. They are the ones who scream,' he answered with a soft lilting voice.

Thor could tell this was the singer of the lullaby just from the way the cat spoke.

'Who are you, then?' demanded Thor, still whispering, but with as much authority as he could manage.

The cat was pleased that this Thunder God was not waking the kittens and his smile broadened even more.

'I am Cat Bayun. These are my children, who scream so loud when they are tired and hungry.'

'But where is their mother?' asked Thor, looking about.

Cat Bayun sighed and his smile dropped a little, 'She gave birth to the two littl'uns and then left me so that she could be the protector of a people who live on the Sandstone Ridge. I am the only one then who feeds these kittens, protects them and tries to get them to sleep.' He then looked nervously down at his two sleeping babies, hoping that this conversation would not wake them.

Thor looked down at the sleeping pair as well and a thought dawned.

'Cat Bayun,' he said, 'these kittens need a mother. Let me take them to the goddess Freya. She is fond of cats and she would welcome them into her home. She would look after them for you and they would be the wards of a goddess.'

Thor knew immediately that Freya would prefer two furry blue kittens to a wet dragon in a net.

The father cat looked at his two youngsters, then back at the Thunder God with his head on one side. This was a big decision and his smile disappeared completely as he considered the offer.

'Come, come,' demanded Thor, 'I need a decision. If you will not let me take the kittens, then I have a dragon to catch.'

Thor's impatience made him forget to whisper, and his deep voice boomed around the trees like thunder. The two blue kittens awoke suddenly and started crying again with their sharp, squealing voices.

Cat Bayun was certainly not smiling now.

'See what you have done, you blundering fool!' he spat at Thor.

'What?' bellowed the Thunder God, 'You talk to me like that? Why you insolent mug of a moggy!' And he reached out to grab that cat off the tree, to teach him some manners.

But suddenly, Cat Bayun disappeared. In a split second, tail, body and head evaporated and Thor was left simply grasping the air. Then there was a rustling in the leaves and a grey and black bird seemed to take to the air above. Was this Cat Bayun in a new shape?

As Thor looked up and saw the bird disappear into the distant sky, he was aware of the screaming kittens still at his feet. Their father had now gone and he still needed a gift for Freya. So, taking his cloak and wrapping it about his head to cover his ears, he reached down to the two bundles of blue fur and took them back with him to Asgard.

Freya was delighted with the gift and the two cats remained with her, growing into fine, strong creatures. She was so keen to keep them with her and they loved her company too, that she found a way for the two blue cats to journey with her wherever she should go. And so Freya, the Goddess of Love, travels throughout Asgard, and occasionally down on to Midgard, as a proud and beautiful goddess with Brisingamen around her neck, and the children of Cat Bayun pulling her chariot.

ENIGMATIC SMILES

The previous eight tales have all been about things that happened in years long gone, but in more recent years some intriguing accounts have surfaced which are retellings of more ancient whispers. But before this final story, let us consider the most memorable attributes of the Cheshire Cat. Firstly, it has a large grin. It can disappear and reappear anywhere at will, and even make parts of its body disappear to leave a head floating in mid-air, or simply its smile. So, what about the colour of its fur? Disney popularised the image of the purple cat, but the inn signs around the county show the Cheshire Cat as being golden. Now, bearing all this in mind, let's consider these more modern tales.

In the early 1980s, a farmer at Crewood Hall Farm, outside of Kingsley, claimed that while he was looking out across the fields to the woods on its boundaries, he saw what appeared to be a large, golden cat, creep out from amongst the trees. With gun in hand, he pursued the beast, but it withdrew into the woodland and disappeared, leaving no trace when the farmer reached the spot. Not even a paw print!

A few years earlier, reports had come into the police of a lioness which had been seen about Upton, outside of Chester. The police had gone to investigate but found no such creature and no tracks. The police contacted Chester Zoo, but the zoo authorities said that there were no big cats missing from their enclosures. In fact, no animals were missing, although it is hard to tell with the very small ones.

Every so often reports are made of sightings of a creature in Delamere Forest. The size of the beast varies, but it has been known as the Thing of Delamere. This raises some questions:

Was the golden cat at Kingsley and the lioness at Upton the same beast?

Is it now hiding in Delamere Forest?

If it can disappear without leaving a trace, then is this something more magical than simply an escaped lion?

Is it an older, more mystical, creature – a spirit in the form of a golden cat – the ancient guardian of this mystifying landscape bearing its fangs – the real Cheshire Cat?

Bibliography

Armitage, S., *Sir Gawain and the Green Knight* (Faber & Faber, 2007)

Arrowsmith, N., *Field Guide to the Little People* (Llewellyn, 2009)

Baker, M., *Folklore and Customs of Rural England* (David & Charles, 1975)

Bate, H., Bawn, W., Dakin, R. & Shadbolt, C., *A Local History of Broxton, Duckington & Harthill* (Local Heritage initiative, 2000)

Berry, G., *A History of Grappenhall Church* (Grappenhall Church, 2000)

Bevan, R.M. & Coxhead, A.D., *The Story of Delamere House and Delamere Park* (CC Publishing, 2008)

Bowerman, T., *Walks in Mysterious Cheshire and Wirral* (Northern Eye Books, 2006)

Bowerman, T., *Walking Cheshire's Sandstone Trail* (Northern Eye Books, 2008)

Carroll, L., *Alice's Adventures in Wonderland* (Everyman's Library, 1992)

Clay, R.M., *The Hermits and Anchorites of England* (Methuen & Co., 1914)

Clinging, R., *Cheshire Folk Songs and Associated Traditions* (Leonie Press, 2005)

Coward, I.A., *Cheshire – Traditions and History* (Methuen & Co., 1932)

Dore, R.N., *Cheshire* (B.T. Batsford, 1976)

Douglasson, H., *Wirral Vikings – The Wider Context* (Countyvise Ltd, 2005)

Edwards, J.F., *Village Walks in Cheshire* (Countryside Books, 1997)

Ellison, N., *The Wirral Peninsula* (Robert Hale Ltd, 1973)

Garner, A., *The Weirdstone of Brisingamen* (Harper Collins, 2010)

Green, R.L., *The Adventures of Robin Hood* (Everyman's Library, 1994)

Harding, S., *Ingimund's Saga – Norwegian Wirral* (Countyvise Ltd, 2006)

Hayhurst, A., *Cheshire Murders* (The History Press, 2006)

Haynes, D. (ed), *Burwardsley – The View from the Hill* (Burdwarsley Book Committee, 2000)

Hole, C., *Traditions and Customs of Cheshire* (EP Publishing Ltd, 1970)
Hughes, T., *The Vale Royal of England or the County Palatine of Chester* (E.J. Morten, 1656)
Latham, F.B., *The History of an English Village* (Bunbury Local History Group, 1989)
Leach, J., *Knutsford – A History* (Phillimore, 2007)
Leigh, E., *Ballads and Legends of Cheshire* (Longmans & Co., 1867)
Leigh, E., *A Glossary of Words Used in the Dialect of Cheshire* (Hamilton Adams, 1877)
Newman, J.H., *Lives of the English Saints Volume III* (1901)
Pickford, D., *Cheshire – Its Magic & Mystery* (Sigma Leisure, 1994)
Roberts, P., *Articles in Fabled Felines* (Purr 'n' Fur, 2011)
Rogers, C., *Circular Walks along the Sandstone Trail* (Mara Books, 2006)
Woods, F., *Legends and Traditions of Cheshire* (Shiva Publishing, 1982)
Woods, F., *Further Legends and Traditions of Cheshire* (Shiva Publishing, 1983)
Sexton, C., *Tales of Old Cheshire* (Countryside Books, 2011)
Stephen, R., *The Boom of the Bitterbump – The Folk-history of Cheshire's Wildlife* (Gordon Emery, 2003)
Stoker, R., *The Legacy of Arthur's Chester* (Covenant Publishing, 1965)
Tunstall, B., *The Shiny Night* (Heinemann, 1931)
Walker, J.A.J., *150th Anniversary of the Consecration of St John's Church* (Alvanley Church, 2011)
Wright, T., *St Patrick's Purgatory; An Essay on the Legends of Purgatory, Hell and Paradise Current During the Middle Ages* (John Russell Smith, 1884)

Lightning Source UK Ltd.
Milton Keynes UK
UKOW04f1420090314

227805UK00001B/4/P

9 780752 465135